11·00

KU-197-673

A BARREL OF STORIES FOR SEVEN YEAR OLDS

Also available by Pat Thomson,
and published by Doubleday/Corgi:

A BUS FULL OF STORIES
FOR FOUR YEAR OLDS

A POCKETFUL OF STORIES FOR
FIVE YEAR OLDS

A BUCKETFUL OF STORIES FOR
SIX YEAR OLDS

A BASKET OF STORIES FOR
SEVEN YEAR OLDS

A SACKFUL OF STORIES FOR
EIGHT YEAR OLDS

A CHEST OF STORIES FOR
NINE YEAR OLDS

A SATCHEL OF SCHOOL STORIES

A STOCKING FULL OF CHRISTMAS
STORIES

A CRACKER FULL OF CHRISTMAS STORIES

A BAND OF JOINING-IN STORIES

Of Stories for Seven Year Olds

Collected by
PAT THOMSON

Illustrated by Robin Lawrie

DOUBLEDAY
LONDON · NEW YORK · TORONTO · SYDNEY · AUCKLAND

TRANSWORLD PUBLISHERS LTD
61–63 Uxbridge Road, London W5 5SA

TRANSWORLD PUBLISHERS (AUSTRALIA) PTY LTD
15–25 Helles Avenue, Moorebank, NSW 2170

TRANSWORLD PUBLISHERS (NZ) LTD
3 William Pickering Drive, Albany, Auckland

DOUBLEDAY CANADA LTD
105 Bond Street, Toronto, Ontario M5B 1Y3

Published 1996 by Doubleday
a division of Transworld Publishers Ltd

Collection copyright © 1996 by Pat Thomson
Illustrations copyright © 1996 by Robin Lawrie

The right of Pat Thomson to be identified as the Compiler of this work has been asserted in accordance with the Copyright, Designs and Patents Act 1988

A catalogue record for this book is available from the British Library

ISBN 0 385 40545 6

All rights reserved. No part of this publication may be reproduced, stored in a retrieval system, or transmitted in any form or by any means, electronic, mechanical, photocopying, recording, or otherwise, without the prior permission of the publishers

This book is sold subject to the Standard Conditions of Sale of Net Books and may not be re-sold in the U.K. below the net price fixed by the publishers for the book.

Typeset in 20/26pt Bembo Schoolbook
by Phoenix Typesetting, Ilkley, West Yorkshire

Printed and bound in Great Britain by
Mackays of Chatham PLC, Chatham, Kent

Acknowledgements

The editor and publisher are grateful for permission to include the following copyright material in this anthology:

Joan Aiken, 'The Cost of Night'. From *A Small Pinch of Weather*. First published by Jonathan Cape. Copyright Joan Aiken © 1969. Reprinted by permission of A. M. Heath & Company Limited.

Ruth Ainsworth, 'The Cat Visitor'. From *Ten Tales of Shellover*. First published by Deutsch, 1963. Copyright Ruth Ainsworth © 1963. Reprinted by permission of Scholastic Books.

Ann Cameron, 'A Day When Frogs Wear Shoes'. From *More Stories Julian Tells*. First published by Victor Gollancz Ltd, 1986. Copyright Ann Cameron © 1986. Reprinted by permission of Victor Gollancz.

Anna Fienberg, 'Ignatius Binz and his Magnificent Nose'. From *The Magnificent Nose and Other Marvels*. Published by Oxford University Press, 1991. Copyright Anna Fienberg © 1991. Reprinted by permission of Allen & Unwin.

Adèle Geras, 'The Faces of the Czar'. From *My Grandmother's Stories*. First published by Heinemann, 1990. Copyright Adèle Geras © 1990. Reprinted by permission of Laura Cecil Literary Agency.

Margaret Joy, 'Hallowe'en'. From *You're in the Juniors Now*. First published by Faber and Faber, 1988. Copyright Margaret Joy © 1988. Reprinted by permission of Faber and Faber Ltd.

Dick King-Smith, 'Friends and Brothers'. From *Friends and Brothers*. First published by Heinemann, 1987. Copyright Dick King-Smith © 1987. Reprinted by permission of A. P. Watt Ltd, on behalf of Dick King-Smith.

Sheila Lavelle, 'Sticky Trick'. From *My Best Fiend*. First published by Hamish Hamilton, 1979. Copyright Sheila Lavelle © 1979. Reprinted by permission of Penguin Books.

Ruth Manning-Sanders, 'Esben and the Witch'. From *A Book of Witches*. First published by Methuen, 1965. Copyright Ruth Manning-Sanders © 1965. Reprinted by permission of David Higham Associates.

Ursula Moray Williams, 'A Picnic With The Aunts'. From *Bad Boys*, compiled by Eileen Colwell. First published by Longman Books, 1972. Reprinted by permission of Curtis Brown Ltd, London on behalf of Ursula Moray Williams. Copyright Ursula Moray Williams © 1972.

Philippa Pearce, 'What the Neighbours Did'. From *What the Neighbours Did and Other Stories*. First published by Longman Books, 1972. Copyright Philippa Pearce © 1972. Reprinted by permission of Penguin Books.

Michael Rosen, 'The Silly Ghosts Gruff'. From *Hairy Tales and Nursery Crimes*. First published by Deutsch, 1985. Copyright Michael Rosen © 1985. Reprinted by permission of Scholastic Children's Books.

CONTENTS

Friends and Brothers

'You say that word just once more,' said William to Charlie, 'and I'll hit you.'

Charlie said it.

William hit him.

Charlie then let out a screech and kicked William on the shin, and William bellowed.

William and Charlie's mother came rushing in like a whirlwind, with a face like thunder.

'You two will drive me mad!' she stormed. 'All you do is fight, all day long!'

'William hit me,' said Charlie.

'Why did you hit him, William?'

'Because Charlie keeps on saying the same word.

Whatever I say, he says the same word over and over again. Anyway, he kicked me.'

'Will hit me first,' said Charlie.

'William,' said his mother, 'you are not to hit Charlie. He is younger than you and much smaller. The next time you do, I shall hit you.'

'You didn't ought to, Mum,' said William.

'Why not?'

'I'm younger than you and much smaller.'

'Absolutely,' said Charlie.

'There you are!' shouted William madly. 'That's the word! Whatever I say, he just says "Absolutely". He doesn't even know what it means.'

'Absolutely,' said Charlie.

William let out a yell of rage and rushed at his brother with his fists clenched. Charlie dodged behind his mother, who held the furious William at arm's length.

'Now *stop* it, the pair of you!' she said. 'William, you stop attacking Charlie, and Charlie, you stop annoying Will. I cannot stand one more minute of being shut in this house with you two. Get your bikes. We'll go to the park.'

William stumped off, limping slightly from the kick, and shouting angrily, 'It's not fair!'

From behind his mother's back, Charlie's face appeared. Silently he mouthed the word 'Absolutely'.

In the park, William rode his BMX at top speed. He felt the need to be all by himself, miles from anybody. The roads in the park were full of steep switchback slopes, and William swooped down them flat out. Like a lot of elder brothers, he felt he had had a raw deal.

Charlie, meanwhile, was trying to see how slowly he could pedal without falling off. He had not long inherited William's old bike and was fascinated by the problems of balance. This was much more fun than a tricycle. Like a lot of younger brothers, he had forgotten all about the recent row, and was singing happily to himself. Then he came to the top of one of the steepest slopes. He grinned, and bent low over the handlebars.

His mother, walking some way behind, saw the small figure disappear from view. A moment later, a dreadful wailing started her running hard.

Halfway down the slope, Charlie lay sprawled in the road, the old bike beside him, one wheel still spinning. His face, she saw when she reached him, was covered in blood. There was a deep cut across his forehead and a set of long scratches, gravel-studded, down one cheek.

At that moment William came flying back down the reverse slope and skidded to a halt, wide-eyed with horror at the scene.

'What happened?' he said miserably.

'I don't know. He must have touched the brake and gone straight over the handlebars. Listen carefully, Will. We must get him to hospital quickly – that cut's going to need stitches. I'm going to carry him to the nearest park gate, that one over

there, and try and stop a car to give us a lift. Can you wheel both bikes and stick them out of sight in those bushes, and then run and catch me up?'

'Yes, Mum,' said William.

He looked at his brother's face. Charlie was still crying, but quietly now.

'He'll be all right, won't he?' William said.

Twenty-four hours later, Charlie, recovered now from the shock of the accident, was jabbering away nineteen to the dozen.

He remembered little of the actual crash, or of his treatment in hospital, the stitching of the cut and the cleaning-up of his gravelly face. It was very swollen now, so that one side of him didn't look like Charlie at all, but his voice was as loud and piercing as ever as he plied his brother with endless questions.

'Did you see me come off, Will?'

'No.'

'I went right over the handlebars, didn't I?'

'Suppose so.'

'How fast d'you think I was going, Will?'

'I don't know.'

'A hundred miles an hour, d'you think?' squeaked Charlie excitedly.

'I expect so, Charles,' said William in a kindly

voice. 'You looked an awful mess when I got there.'

'Lots of blood, Will?'

'Yes. Ugh, it was horrible.'

'Then what happened?'

'Well, Mum ran all the way to the nearest gate carrying you, and a kind lady in a car stopped and gave us all a lift to the hospital.'

'And then they stitched me up!' said Charlie proudly.

'Yes.'

'Did you see them stitching me up, Will?'

'No, Charles.'

'I expect it was a huge great needle,' said Charlie happily. 'You've never had six stitches have you, Will?'

'No,' said William. 'You were jolly brave, Charlie,' he said. 'You can have a go on my BMX when you're better.'

'I can't reach the pedals,' Charlie said.

'Oh. Well, you can take a picture with my Instamatic if you like.'

'Can I really, Will?'

'And you can borrow my Swiss Army knife for a bit.'

'Can I really?'

'Yes,' said William. He put his hand in his pocket

and pulled out a rather squidgy-looking bar of chocolate.

'And you can have half of this,' he said.

'Gosh, thanks, Will!'

William and Charlie's mother put her head round the door, wondering at the unaccustomed silence, and saw her sons sitting side by side on

Charlie's bed, chewing chocolate. William actually had his arm round Charlie's shoulders.

'Look what I've got, Mum,' said Charlie with his mouth full.

'Did you give him some of yours, Will?' said his mother.

'Naturally,' said William loftily. 'We're friends and brothers.'

Another day went by, and Charlie was definitely better. His face was much less swollen, his spirits high, his voice shriller yet.

He had made up a song about his exploits, which he sang, endlessly and very loudly.

'Who came rushing down the hill?
Charlie boy!
Who had such an awful spill?
Charlie boy!
Who came down with a terrible thud,
Covered in mud and covered in blood?
Charlie, Charlie, Charlie boy!'

William, as he occasionally did, had an attack of earache, painful enough without Charlie's singing.

'Charles,' he said as the friend and brother was

just about to come rushing down the hill for the twentieth time, 'd'you think you could keep a bit quiet?'

'Why?' shouted Charlie at the top of his voice.

'Because I've got earache.'

'Oh,' said Charlie in a whisper. 'Oh, sorry, Will. Does it hurt a lot?'

'Yes,' said William, white-faced, 'it does.'

For the rest of the day Charlie tiptoed about the house, occasionally asking William if he needed anything, and, if he did, fetching it. He guarded his brother's peace and quiet fiercely, frowning angrily at his mother when she dropped a saucepan on the kitchen floor.

'Hullo, Charlie boy!' shouted his father on his return from work. 'How's the poor old face?'

'Don't make such a noise, Dad!' hissed Charlie furiously. 'Will's got earache.'

It was now a week since Charlie's accident, a week of harmony and brotherly love.

Charlie's face was now miles better and William's earache quite gone.

They were drawing pictures, at the kitchen table, with felt pens.

'Charles,' said William. 'Can I borrow your red? Mine's run out.'

'No,' said Charlie.

'Why not? You're not using it.'

'Yes, I am,' said Charlie, picking up his red felt and colouring with it.

'You just did that to be annoying,' said William angrily.

The word 'annoying' rang a bell with Charlie, and he grinned and nodded and said 'Absolutely!'

'Charlie!' said William between his teeth. 'Don't start that again or I'll hit you!'

'You can't,' said Charlie. 'I've got a bad face.'

'I'll hit you all the same,' said William.

'I'll shout in your bad ear,' said Charlie, 'and d'you know what I'll shout?'

'What?'

'ABSOLUTELY!!' yelled Charlie and scuttled out of the room with William in hot pursuit, as life returned to normal.

This story is by Dick King-Smith.

A Picnic with the Aunts

There were once six lucky, lucky boys who were invited by their aunts to go on a picnic expedition to an island in the middle of a lake.

The boys' names were Freddie, Adolphus, Edward, Montague, Montmorency and little John Henry. Their aunts were Aunt Bossy, Aunt Millicent, Aunt Celestine, Aunt Miranda, Aunt Adelaide and Auntie Em.

The picnic was to be a great affair, since the lake was ten miles off, and they were to drive there in a wagonette pulled by two grey horses. Once arrived at the lake they were to leave the wagonette and get into a rowing-boat with all the provisions for the picnic, also umbrellas, in case it rained. The aunts were bringing cricket bats, stumps and balls for the boys to play with, and a rope for them to jump over. There was also a box of fireworks to let off at the close of the day when it was getting dark, before they all got into the boat and rowed back to the shore. The wagonette with Davy Driver would leave them at the lake in the morning and come back to fetch them in the evening, at nine o'clock.

The food for the picnic was quite out of this world, for all the aunts were excellent cooks.

There were strawberry tarts, made by Aunt Bossy, and gingerbread covered with almonds baked by Aunt Millicent. Aunt Celestine had prepared a quantity of sausage rolls, while Aunt Miranda's cheese tarts were packed in a tea cosy to keep them warm. Aunt Adelaide had cut so many sandwiches they had to be packed in a suitcase, while Auntie Em had supplied ginger pop, and apples, each one polished like a looking glass on the back of her best serge skirt.

Besides the provisions the aunts had brought their embroidery and their knitting, a book of fairy tales in case the boys were tired, a bottle of physic in case they were ill, and a cane in case they were naughty. And they had invited the boys' headmaster, Mr Hamm, to join the party, as company for themselves and to prevent their nephews from becoming too unruly.

The wagonette called for the boys at nine o'clock in the morning – all the aunts were wearing their best Sunday hats, and the boys had been forced by

their mother into their best sailor suits. When Mr Headmaster Hamm had been picked up, the party was complete, only he had brought his fiddle with him and the wagonette was really very overcrowded. At each hill the boys were forced to get out and walk, which they considered very unfair, for their headmaster was so fat he must have weighed far more than the six of them put together, but they arrived at the lake at last.

There was a great unpacking of aunts and provisions, a repetition of orders to Davy Driver, and a scolding of little boys, who were running excitedly towards the water's edge with knitting wool wound about their ankles.

A large rowing-boat was moored to a ring on the shore. When it was loaded with passengers and provisions it looked even more overcrowded than the wagonette had done, but Aunt Bossy seized an oar and Mr Headmaster Hamm another – Auntie Em took a third, while two boys manned each of the remaining three.

Amid much splashing and screaming the boat moved slowly away from the shore and inched its way across the lake to the distant island, the boys crashing their oars together while Auntie Em and Aunt Bossy grew pinker and pinker in the face as they strove to keep up with Mr Headmaster

Hamm, who rowed in his shirt sleeves, singing the Volga Boat Song.

It was a hot summer's day. The lake lay like a sheet of glass, apart from the long ragged wake behind the boat. Since they all had their backs to the island they hit it long before they realized they had arrived, and the jolt crushed Aunt Millicent's legs between the strawberry tarts and the ginger-beer bottles.

The strawberry jam oozed on to her shins convincing her that she was bleeding to death. She lay back fainting in the arms of Mr Headmaster Hamm, until little John Henry remarked that Aunt Millicent's blood looked just like his favourite jam, whereupon she sat up in a minute, and told him that he was a very disgusting little boy.

Aunt Bossy decided that the boat should be tied up in the shade of some willow trees and the provisions left inside it to keep cool until dinner-time. The boys were very disappointed, for they were all hungry and thought it must be long past dinner-time already.

'You boys can go and play,' Aunt Bossy told them. She gave them the cricket stumps, the bat and ball, and the rope to jump over, but they did not want to jump or play cricket. They wanted to rush about the island and explore, to look for birds' nests and to climb trees, to play at cowboys and Indians and to swim in the lake.

But all the aunts began to make aunt-noises at once:

'Don't get too hot!'

'Don't get too cold!'

'Don't get dirty!'

'Don't get wet!'

'Keep your hats on or you'll get sunstroke!'

'Keep your shoes on or you'll cut your feet!'

'Keep out of the water or you'll be drowned!'

'Don't fight!'

'Don't shout!'

'Be good!'

'Be good!'

'Be good!'

'There! You hear what your aunts say,' added Mr Headmaster Hamm. 'So mind you are good!'

The six aunts and Mr Headmaster Hamm went to sit under the trees to knit and embroider and play the fiddle, leaving the boys standing on the shore, looking gloomily at one another.

'Let's not,' said Adolphus.

'But if we aren't,' said Edward, 'we shan't get any dinner.'

'Let's have dinner first,' suggested little John Henry.

They sat down on the grass above the willow trees looking down on the boat. It was a long time since breakfast and they could not take their eyes off the boxes of provisions tucked underneath the seats, the bottle of ginger pop restored to order, and Auntie Em's basket of shining, rosy apples.

Voices came winging across the island:

'Why are you boys sitting there doing nothing at all? Why can't you find something nice to do on this lovely island?'

Quite coldly and firmly Freddie stood up and faced his brothers.

'Shall we leave them to it?' he suggested.

'What do you mean?' cried Adolphus, Edward, Montague, Montmorency and little John Henry.

'We'll take the boat and the provisions and row away to the other end of the lake, leaving them behind!' said Freddie calmly.

'Leave them behind on the island!' his brothers echoed faintly.

As the monstrous suggestion sank into their minds all six boys began to picture the fun they might have if they were free of the aunts and of Mr Headmaster Hamm. As if in a dream they followed Freddie to the boat, stepped inside and cast off the rope. At the very last moment Adolphus flung the suitcase of sandwiches ashore before each boy seized an oar and rowed for their lives away from the island.

By the time the six aunts and Mr Headmaster Hamm had realized what was happening the boat was well out into the lake, and the boys took not the slightest notice of the waving handkerchiefs, the calls, the shouts, the pleadings and even the bribes that followed them across the water.

It was a long, hard pull to the end of the lake but not a boy flagged until the bows of the boat touched shore and the island was a blur in the far distance. Then, rubbing the blistered palms of their hands, they jumped ashore, tying the rope to a rock, and tossing the provisions from one to another in a willing chain.

Then began the most unforgettable afternoon of their lives. It started with a feast, when each boy stuffed himself with whatever he fancied most. Ginger-beer bottles popped and fizzed, apple cores were tossed far and wide. When they had finished eating they amused themselves by writing impolite little messages to their aunts and to Mr Headmaster Hamm, stuffing them into the empty bottles and sending them off in the direction of the little island.

They wrote such things as:

'Hey diddle diddle,
Old Ham and his fiddle
Sharp at both ends
And flat in the middle!'

'Aunt Miranda has got so thin
She has got nothing to keep her inside in.'

'My Aunt Boss rides a hoss.
Which is boss, hoss or Boss?'

Fortunately, since they forgot to replace the stoppers, all the bottles went to the bottom long before they reached their goal.

After this they swam in the lake, discovering enough mud and weeds to plaster themselves with dirt until they looked like savages. Drying themselves on the trousers of their sailor suits they dressed again and rushed up into the hills beyond the lake where they discovered a cave, and spent an enchanting afternoon playing at robbers, and hurling great stones down the steep hillside.

Feeling hungry again the boys ate the rest of the provisions, and then, too impatient to wait for the dark, decided to let off the box of fireworks. Even by daylight these provided a splendid exhibition as Freddie lit one after another. Then a spark fell on

Montague's collar, burning a large hole, while Montmorency burnt his hand and hopped about crying loudly. To distract him Freddie lit the largest rocket of all, which they had been keeping for the last.

They all waited breathlessly for it to go off, watching the little red spark creep slowly up the twist of paper until it reached the vital spot. With a tremendous hiss the rocket shot into the air. Montmorency stopped sucking his hand and all the boys cheered.

But the rocket hesitated and faltered in mid-flight. It turned a couple of somersaults in the air and dived straight into the boat, landing in the bows with a crash.

Before it could burn the wood or do any damage Freddie rushed after it. With a prodigious bound he leapt into the boat that had drifted a few yards from the shore.

Unfortunately he landed so heavily that his foot went right through one of the boards, and although he seized the stick of the rocket and hurled it far into the lake, the water came through the hole so quickly that the fire would have been quenched in any case.

There was nothing that any of them could do, for the boat was rotten, and the plank had simply

given way. They were forced to stand and watch it sink before their eyes in four feet of water.

The sun was setting now. The surrounding hills threw blue shadows into the lake. A little breeze sprang up ruffling the water. The island seemed infinitely far away.

Soberly, sadly, the six boys began to walk down the shore to the beginning of the lake, not knowing what they would do when they got there. They were exhausted by their long, mad afternoon – some were crying and others limping.

Secretly the younger ones hoped that when they arrived they would find the grown-ups waiting for them, but when they reached the beginning of the lake no grown-ups were there. Not even Davy Driver.

'We will build a fire!' Freddie announced to revive their spirits. 'It will keep us warm and show the aunts we are all safe and well.'

'They get so anxious about us!' said Montmorency.

So they built an enormous bonfire from all the driftwood and dry branches they could find. This cheered them all very much because they were strictly forbidden to make bonfires at home.

It was dark by now, but they had the fire for light, and suddenly the moon rose, full and stately, flooding the lake with a sheet of silver. The boys laughed and shouted. They flung more branches on to the fire and leapt up and down.

Suddenly Adolphus stopped in mid-air and pointed, horror-struck, towards the water.

Far out on the silver lake, sharply outlined against the moonlight, they saw a sight that froze their blood to the marrow.

It was the aunts' hats, drifting towards the shore.

The same little breeze that rippled the water and fanned their fire was blowing the six hats away from the island, and as they floated closer and closer to the shore the boys realized for the first time what a terrible thing they had done, for kind Aunt Bossy, generous Aunt Millicent, good Aunt Celestine, devoted Aunt Miranda, worthy Aunt Adelaide and dear, *dear* Auntie Em, together with their much respected headmaster, Mr Hamm, had all been DROWNED!

Freddie, Adolphus, Edward, Montague, Montmorency and little John Henry burst into tears of such genuine repentance and grief that it would have done their aunts good to hear them. They sobbed so bitterly that after a while they had no more tears left to weep, and it was little John Henry who first wiped his eyes on his sleeve and recovered his composure. The next moment his mouth opened wide and his eyes seemed about to burst out of his head.

He pointed a trembling finger towards the lake and all his brothers looked where he was pointing. Then their eyes bulged too and their mouths dropped open as they beheld the most extraordinary sight they had ever dreamed of.

The aunts were swimming home!

For under the hats there were heads, and behind the heads small wakes of foam bore witness to the efforts of the swimmers.

The hats were perfectly distinguishable. First came Aunt Bossy's blue hydrangeas topped by a purple bow, then Aunt Millicent's little lilac bonnet. Close behind Aunt Millicent came Aunt Celestine's boater, smartly ribboned in green plush, followed by Aunt Miranda's black velvet toque, with a bunch of violets. Then some yards farther from the shore a floral platter of pansies and roses that Aunt Adelaide had bought to open a Church Bazaar. And last of all came Auntie Em in her pink straw pillbox hat, dragging behind her with a rope the picnic suitcase, on which was seated Mr Headmaster Hamm, who could not swim.

Holding the sides of the suitcase very firmly with both hands, he carried between his teeth, as a dog carries a most important bone, the aunts' cane.

Motionless and petrified, with terror and relief boiling together in their veins, Freddie, Adolphus, Edward, Montague, Montmorency and little John Henry stood on the shore – the fire shining on their filthy suits, dirty faces and sodden shoes, while slowly, steadily, the aunts swam back from the island, and far behind them over the hills appeared at last the lights of Davy Driver's wagonette, coming to fetch them home.

This story is by Ursula Moray Williams.

Sticky Trick

Playing tricks on people is Angela's favourite hobby. She even does it to me sometimes, and I'm supposed to be her best friend. Once she rushed into our house shouting 'Charlie! Quick! Come and see! There's a man walking down the street with no trousers on!' I went dashing out to have a look, but it was only Mr MacLennon in his kilt, and Angela fell about laughing when she saw my face. My dad thought it was funny too, but my mum said Angela was a very rude girl.

Angela does things like that all the time, so it's not really surprising that I thought her laryngitis was just another one of her jokes. It was a Monday morning, and when she called for me on the way to school she had her neck all muffled up in a woolly scarf. I asked her what was the matter, but she could only talk in a hoarse sort of whisper and she told me she'd lost her voice.

Well, I looked at her and all I did was laugh. I was certain it was a trick, especially after what had happened on Friday, so I'd better tell you about that first.

That Friday had been a bad day for Angela, because she was in one of her talkative moods and you know how that always gets on teachers' nerves. My dad says that when Angela is in one of her talkative moods she's even worse than her mother. Anyway, Miss Bennett had to keep on telling her to shut up all day long, and by the last lesson, which was Nature Study, everybody was getting a bit fed up.

We were doing the Life History of the Frog, and the trouble was that Angela knew it all already. In fact the whole class knew it all already because we'd done the Life History of the Frog last year in Mrs Moody's class and the year before in Miss Whiteman's *and* the year before that in Miss Spender's, and it seems to me that you have to do the Life History of the Frog in every class in every school from the Kindergarten to the Sixth Form.

Teachers get ever so flustered and upset if you say you've done it before so you have to let them get on with it and pretend it's all new and interesting. But I don't mind doing it all over again because I like drawing those funny little tadpoles with their wiggly tails and I'm getting quite good at them now.

Anyway, Miss Bennett had some baby tadpoles in a jar and she was holding them up in front of the class while she talked so that we could all see them.

'And then, after the eggs hatch out,' she said, 'the tadpoles feed on the jelly around them.' Angela bobbed up out of her chair.

'Please, Miss Bennett,' she said. 'I saw this programme on the telly the other day. And the man said they don't think that's true any more. Everybody used to think so, but now they've found out that the jelly is only a sort of protection, and the baby tadpoles feed on pondweed and possibly small organizations in the water.'

Miss Bennett sighed. 'I think you mean organisms, Angela,' she said. Angela nodded and sat down.

'Well, that's most interesting,' continued Miss Bennett. 'You can see how science is discovering new facts all the time. Now, where was I? Oh, yes.

The young tadpoles breathe under water by means of—'

'Gills,' said Angela, bouncing out of her desk again. 'They're very interesting things, Miss Bennet, because they can absorb oxygen from the water.'

Miss Bennett frowned. 'That's quite correct, Angela,' she said. 'I'm glad you know so much about it. But I'd rather you didn't interrupt the lesson. There'll be plenty of time for discussion afterwards.' Miss Bennett looked down at the jar of tadpoles.

'Now, the hind legs develop first, and then the—' But Angela was on her feet again.

'I'm sorry, Miss Bennett,' she said. 'But the man on the telly said that all the legs develop at the same time. It only looks as if the hind legs develop first, because the front ones are hidden by the gill flaps.'

'Angela!' said Miss Bennett crossly. 'I have asked you not to interrupt. If it happens again I shall have to send you out of the room. I don't know what's the matter with you today.' Miss Bennett started to walk around the room, stopping at each desk to show us the tadpoles in the jar.

'This is the stage these tadpoles are at now,' she went on. 'They are growing very rapidly and need lots of food. We can even give them small pieces of meat to nibble and—'

'Excuse me, Miss Bennett,' said Angela, jumping up yet again. 'But when we were in Miss Spender's class, Miss Spender said . . . '

Miss Bennett slammed the jar of tadpoles down on my desk with such a crash that some of the water slopped over the top. I watched the tadpoles wriggling with fright and I knew just how they felt.

'Angela Mitchell!' snapped Miss Bennett. 'I don't want to hear one more word from you today. You will please stand outside the door for the remainder of the lesson. And when you go home you will write out fifty times, "I must not speak until I'm spoken to" and bring it to me on Monday morning.'

I could tell by Angela's face that she was furious. Her mouth went all sulky and she stalked out of the room. I even thought she was going to slam the door, but there are some things that even Angela daren't do. She was still furious when school finished for the day and we started walking home together.

'That Miss Bennett is an old cat,' she muttered, with a scowl. 'I'm never going to speak to her again. Not ever!'

'Oh, Angela,' I said. 'You don't really mean

that.' Angela stamped her foot in temper and pushed me away from her.

'You're pathetic,' she said. 'I most certainly do mean it. And if you were a proper sort of friend, YOU wouldn't speak to her again EITHER!'

We went home and I didn't see Angela at all on Saturday or Sunday because my mum and dad and I drove up to Newcastle that night to stay with my grandma, and she's my dad's mother and she's kind and fat and cuddly and she bakes the best stottie cakes in the North East. We didn't get back until very late on Sunday evening, so the next time I saw Angela was on Monday morning. And that was when she came round and told me she'd lost her voice.

Well, can you blame me if I didn't believe her? I looked at her suspiciously, and she had that sparkly look in her eyes that always means she's up to something.

'You haven't really lost your voice,' I said. 'Not really and truly. It's a trick. It's just so you won't have to talk to Miss Bennett, isn't it?' But she shook her head and pointed into her mouth.

'Laryngitis,' she whispered, and gave a husky sort of giggle, and I started to giggle too. I thought it was the funniest joke she had ever thought of, and I couldn't wait to see what happened when she tried it out on Miss Bennett.

So off we went to school and the first thing Miss Bennett said when we went into the classroom after prayers was 'Well, Angela? Did you do your lines?'

Angela smiled politely and nodded her head. She opened her satchel and put some sheets of paper on Miss Bennett's desk.

'Thank you, Angela,' said Miss Benett. 'I hope this has taught you a lesson. We'll say no more about it, but I would like you to promise that it won't happen again.'

Angela opened and shut her mouth once or twice and made a funny little croaking sound. I had to stuff my hanky in my mouth to stop myself from laughing when she solemnly shook her head and pointed her finger down her throat.

'Can't . . .' she whispered. 'Can't talk.'

'Oh, dear,' said Miss Bennett. 'What's the matter, Angela? Have you lost your voice or something?' Angela nodded hard and Miss Bennett gave her a sympathetic little smile.

'Well, I'm sorry to hear that,' she said. 'But at least it means we'll all get some peace and quiet for a couple of days.' Everybody laughed when Miss Bennett said that, because it was a joke, and you always have to laugh at teachers' jokes. Angela went to her seat, blushing and scowling, and I heard Laurence Parker hiss 'Dummy!' at her as she went past.

'And now let's get on with our poetry lesson,' said Miss Bennett. 'We've wasted enough time this morning. I hope you've all learnt your poem over the weekend. Charlotte, will you please stand up and recite the first few lines of Wordsworth's "Daffodils".'

I got up and took a quick peep over my shoulder at Angela. And then I suddenly went cold all over because she was staring at me in a funny sort of way and telling me something with her eyes. I knew what she wanted me to do. She wanted me to prove that I was a proper sort of friend. She wanted me to pretend that I'd lost my voice too, so that I wouldn't have to speak to Miss Bennett either.

'Well, come along, Charlotte,' said Miss Bennett impatiently. 'You haven't forgotten it, surely.'

I gazed miserably down at my desk and thought if Angela was brave enough to do it then I must be too, or she would never forgive me. She would choose somebody else to be her best friend and it would probably be that awful Delilah Jones. I opened my mouth.

'I wandered lonely . . .' I whispered, and then stopped.

Miss Bennett stared at me suspiciously.

'What's the matter?' she said in a stern voice.

I pointed down my throat and shook my head, just as Angela had done. Miss Bennett looked from me to Angela and then back again.

'Charlotte Ellis!' she said sharply. 'This is quite ridiculous! You can't mean that you've lost your voice, too?' I nodded dumbly and Miss Bennett's face went pink and some of the boys started to snigger.

'I'm afraid I find this very hard to believe,' said Miss Bennett icily. 'That you should both happen to lose your voices on the same day. I don't suppose either of you has a note from your doctor?'

I shook my head again and looked at Angela, expecting her to do the same. Now we're for it, I thought. But Angela was rummaging in her satchel and then I couldn't believe my eyes because she got out a small white envelope and took it to Miss Bennett with a polite smile. My heart sank into a big heavy lump at the bottom of my stomach.

Miss Bennett opened the envelope and read the note.

'This is indeed from Angela's doctor,' she said. 'It explains that Angela has a mild throat ailment and has lost her voice. It says that it is not serious or infectious, however, and she is quite well enough

to attend school providing she stays indoors at break times.' Miss Bennett folded the note and glared at me over the top of her glasses.

'Well, Charlotte? I suppose you have a note from your doctor?'

I swallowed and croaked weakly, 'No, Miss Bennett.'

'And in fact you haven't lost your voice at all,' said Miss Bennett in an ominous sort of way.

I hung my head. 'No, Miss Bennett,' I said.

'Then what is your explanation for this strange behaviour?'

'It was . . . it was a joke,' I mumbled. Everybody tittered and giggled and Miss Bennett looked round the room with a stern expression.

'I'm afraid none of us find that sort of joke in the least amusing, do we?' she said to the class. And they all stopped sniggering and shook their heads solemnly, and doesn't it make you sick the way everybody always agrees with the teacher?

'Charlotte, you will stay indoors at break time and clean out the art cupboard as a punishment,' said Miss Bennett. 'And you will please try to behave more sensibly in future.'

'Yes, Miss Bennett. Thank you, Miss Bennett,' I breathed gratefully. Cleaning out the art cupboard is a horrible mucky job and it makes your hands all filthy but it's a lot better than some of the punishments Miss Bennett manages to think up. So I felt I was quite lucky really and I didn't mind too much when everybody else trooped out to play at the end of the lesson. Anyway, it meant that I could stay indoors with Angela, and do you know, she didn't laugh a bit about me making such a right idiot of myself about the laryngitis, and she even started to help me tidy the cupboard. But that was when the other awful thing happened.

I was clearing out all the junk which had been shoved to the back of the cupboard when I came across an old battered tin. I heaved it out and looked at the label and it said Cow Gum. I laughed and showed it to Angela.

'I wonder if that's for sticking cows,' I said. Then I started to put it away again on one of the shelves but Angela leaned over and took it out of my hands. Her face had sort of lighted up and I could see that she'd had one of her wicked ideas.

'What are you doing?' I said anxiously. Angela found a stick and prised off the lid of the tin and we both looked inside. A thick layer of glue lay at the bottom, all sticky and shiny like varnish. Angela gazed at it for a minute, then she skipped away across the room with the tin in her hands. She stopped beside Miss Bennett's chair and started to dip the stick in the glue. I gave a shriek of horror.

'Angela! Don't!' I pleaded. 'Not Miss Bennett's chair!'

Angela turned and waved the stick at me. 'You're right,' she whispered hoarsely. 'I think I'll use it on a pig, instead.' She crossed the room quickly, and before I could even try to stop her she had scraped out a big dollop of glue and spread it all over the seat of Laurence Parker's chair.

She pushed the tin of glue back in the cupboard just in time because that moment the bell rang for the end of break and the other children started to come back into the classroom. That nosy Delilah Jones began to wrinkle her face and sniff as soon as she came into the room.

'What's that funny smell?' she asked. But Angela only shrugged her shoulders and looked blank, and I turned my back and went on putting all the stuff back in the cupboard. I didn't know what else to do.

When I had finished I went back to my place and sat down. I had a quick peep at Laurence Parker's chair and you couldn't tell there was glue on it at all. It only looked a bit more shiny than usual. Then I saw Laurence Parker come into the room so I put my head inside my desk because I just couldn't bear to watch him sit down.

I knew Miss Bennett had come in because all the chattering suddenly stopped and I heard everybody scuttling to their places.

'We're going to do some spelling now,' came Miss Bennett's voice. 'Take out your green spelling books, please, everybody. You may have five minutes to revise the twenty words we did last week, and then I'll test you on them.'

I grabbed my spelling book and when I put down my desk lid I saw that Laurence Parker was sitting in his place next to me and he hadn't noticed a thing. I looked over my shoulder, but Angela had her head down over her book and didn't look up.

It was all quiet for a few minutes while everybody except me practised their words and then Miss Bennett stood up.

‘We’ll start from the front row,’ she said. ‘I’ll ask each of you to spell one word for me. Now, Delilah. You’re first. Your word is, enough.’

And that awful Delilah Jones leaped up, looking all smug and pleased with herself. ‘E,N,O,U,G,H,’ she said, and Miss Bennett smiled at her and said ‘Well done,’ and you should have seen Delilah Jones smirking all over her silly face.

Well, it went all the way along the front row and then all the way along the next row and then it was our row and I started to get that horrible feeling in my stomach that’s called butterflies and I don’t know why it’s called getting butterflies because I think it feels more like great big creepy crawly caterpillars. And it was my turn at last and Miss Bennett said ‘Pneumonia, Charlotte,’ and it was the hardest word on the list and I should have known Miss Bennett would save that one for me. Of course I knew how to spell it. But how could I think straight? How could anybody think straight if they knew that it was Laurence Parker’s turn next and he was sitting there glued to his seat?

I stood up quickly. ‘New what?’ I said stupidly, and Miss Bennett’s mouth went all squeezed up at the corners as if she was sucking a lemon.

‘Pneumonia,’ she said again.

'Um, er, N,E,W . . . ' I began and Laurence Parker gave a snigger.

'Sit down, Charlotte,' said Miss Bennett crossly. 'It's obvious you don't know it. You must write it out three times in your book and learn it for next week. Perhaps Laurence Parker can do better. Laurence? Pneumonia, please.'

There was a sort of horrible clatter as Laurence Parker got to his feet and I didn't know where to look because of course his chair was stuck firmly

to the seat of his trousers and had got up with him. His face went all red and he swung around to try to see what was the matter, but that only made things worse because the legs of the chair crashed into the desk behind. Miss Bennett's face went as black as thunder and everybody stared like anything and there were a few smothered giggles but nobody dared laugh out loud.

'What on earth are you doing, boy?' snapped Miss Bennett and Laurence Parker started twisting about and trying to pull himself free but the chair was well and truly stuck.

'Laurence Parker! Come here AT ONCE!' shouted Miss Bennett. 'I will not tolerate this sort of clowning during my lessons!'

Laurence Parker hunched his shoulders and shuffled forward to the front of the class, clutching the chair to his bottom with his hands. He looked a bit like a fat old tortoise with its house on its back.

'I . . . I seem to have got stuck,' he stammered miserably, and Miss Bennett clucked and tutted and fussed. Then she put one hand on his shoulder and the other on the back of the chair and pulled.

There was a dreadful ripping noise and there stood Miss Bennett looking a bit surprised with the chair in her hand and hanging from the chair was a big piece of grey material. And there stood Laurence Parker looking even more surprised with a great big ragged hole in the seat of his trousers and you could see his blue and red striped Marks and Spencers underwear. Everybody stared in horror and the whole room went dead quiet and all you could hear was people breathing and that was when I started to laugh.

It wouldn't have been so bad if it had been a quiet little giggle, or a subdued sort of chuckle, but it wasn't. It was a horrible loud cackle. My dad says that when I laugh I sound like an old hen laying an egg. And I always seem to laugh at the wrong time and in the wrong place and sometimes it gets me into terrible trouble but I can't help it. Like the time at the vicar's garden party when Miss Menzies sneezed and her false teeth flew out and landed in the bowl of fruit punch. And that other time when we went to my Auntie Fiona's wedding up in Gateshead and my grandad trod on the end of the bride's long white veil as she was walking down the aisle and yanked it clean off her head and I laughed so much that I was sent out of the church and had to wait outside in the car so I missed the whole thing.

Anyway, Laurence Parker looked so funny standing there with that great hole in his trousers that if I hadn't laughed I'd have burst. My eyes streamed with tears and this time it was no use stuffing my hanky in my mouth because it only made me choke and laugh even more. And then of course when I started laughing like that it set everybody else off as well and soon the whole class was laughing like anything and you should have heard the din.

Miss Bennett started to thump on her desk with her fist and I knew I was in bad trouble because she only does that when she's really mad. And when I saw the way she was glaring at me I wished I hadn't laughed so much because of course that was what made her think it was me who had been messing about with the rotten old glue.

'There is glue on this chair,' said Miss Bennett, sort of quietly and ominously. 'And I don't have to ask who is responsible for this outrage.' Her eyes bored into me and I felt my face go scarlet. 'There were only two people left in this room at break time, and one of them has guilt written all over her face.' Miss Bennett turned to Laurence Parker, who had backed up against the wall to hide his underwear and was standing there looking daggers at me.

'Laurence,' she said, quite gently. 'You had better go and wait in the boys' changing room. I'm going to phone your mother and ask her to bring you a spare pair of trousers.' Then she turned back to me and her voice would have frozen the Sahara Desert. 'Charlotte Ellis, you will stay behind after school this afternoon. You and I must have a very serious talk.'

Well, of course I sort of hoped that Angela would stand up and confess, but I must admit I wasn't all that surprised when she didn't because I know what she's like. And I didn't get a single chance to speak to her on her own for the rest of that day, as she had to stay indoors again at lunch time because of her sore throat. So when four o'clock came everybody went home and I had to stay behind and get told off, and it was awful because Miss Bennett went on and on at me until I thought she'd never stop and all I could do was stand there and say nothing because of course she knew that it could only have been me or Angela and I couldn't tell on my friend, could I? Even if she did deserve it.

When at last she had let me go and I escaped out of the school door, who should be waiting for me at the gate but Angela, and she had waited for me in the cold all that time. But when she squeezed my arm and whispered that I was the best friend in the whole world I pressed my lips tight together and walked away from her, because this time she'd gone too far and at least she could have taken a bit of the blame.

And then when I got home I suddenly felt a whole lot better, because my dad was there. And I told him all about it because I always tell my dad everything, and he said I was quite right not to tell on my friend. But he said Angela was a right little minx and it was high time I gave her the push and found myself a new best friend who wouldn't keep getting me into trouble.

I thought about that, and in the end I made up my mind that he was right. I even managed not to speak to Angela for three whole days.

But somehow life is never so much fun without her, and when she came round on the third day, looking as sorry as can be and carrying her favourite picture of Elton John as a peace offering, I couldn't help feeling glad to see her and I hadn't the heart to stay cross with her any longer.

This story is by Sheila Lavelle.

The Cat Visitor

Once upon a time a poor old man was sweeping his floor with a broom, sighing to himself as he swept. 'Oh dear,' he sighed. 'How cold it is tonight! How my back aches when I bend it! How hard life is when you are old and tired and haven't much money!'

'But this is Saturday night,' he thought and smiled, so that his thin, brown face was creased and crumpled like the skin of a withered apple. 'Saturday night, the one night in the week when I have a good supper of meat, and a bowl of bread and milk just before I go to bed. There's nothing like a bowl of bread and milk to warm a man and send him into a sound sleep.'

He was just propping the broom up in its corner, when he thought he heard a faint cry outside the door. The wind was howling in the chimney and the rain was beating on the window, and the cry was so faint that he could not be sure he had really heard it.

He stood still and listened. The cry came again, louder than before. The old man hobbled to the door and opened it a little way. In came a mighty blast of wind and a flurry of rain and a thin, black cat.

She was a miserable-looking creature, with thin legs and a thin body and a tail like a black bootlace. But she had the strength to mew and to rub her wet, cold self round the old man's ankles.

The old man dried his soaking visitor with a towel and went to the cupboard for a jug of milk. He filled a saucer and set it on the floor. The cat sprang to the saucer with a growl and lapped the milk noisily, leaving the saucer white and empty. She did not seem grateful, but mewed louder than before, looking up at the old man's face and then at the cupboard, with large, green eyes.

'Why, you're starving, you poor creature,' said the old man, filling the saucer again and adding a crumbled slice of bread to make the milk more satisfying. The saucer was emptied in a twinkling, and the mewing began once more, louder than ever. Once again the jug was brought out and the saucer filled and more bread added, only to be emptied in a few seconds. The more the cat drank, the thirstier she seemed to get.

'There's hardly enough left for my bread and milk,' thought the old man, peering into the jug, 'and only a crust of bread. She may as well have the lot.' He emptied the jug into the saucer, draining the last drop, and crumbled the crust. When this, too, had vanished, the cat licked her lips and gazed hungrily round the room. Then she lifted her head and sniffed the air. She lashed her tail from side to side. The fur on her back bristled. She could smell the mutton chop that was in the cupboard, the old man's weekly treat.

The piercing mewing began again. The cat scratched at the cupboard door, looked over her shoulder at the old man, and then scratched again as if in a frenzy. Her eyes shone like green lamps. The old man could bear it no longer. He went to the cupboard, opened the door, and cut a piece off one end of the chop and gave it to her. She gulped it down and began to scratch with more energy than before, mewing pitifully.

'We'll go halves, that's fair as I'm hungry too,' said the old man, dividing what was left of the meat into two pieces and giving the cat one. But the cat's half vanished before he could shut the door, and the mewing went on so loudly that the old man gave up his own half to his visitor.

The meat finished, the cat still prowled up and down, mewing and looking up at him. She knew there was still the bone on the shelf. Now the old man had hoped to save at least the bone and boil it up later to make a drop of broth, but he could not shut his ears to the pitiful cries, or shut his eyes against the thin, bootlace of a tail and the great pleading eyes. He gave her the bone and she pounced on it and gnawed it with her sharp teeth, till it, too, was gone.

Then, at last, the mewing stopped as if the cat knew there was nothing left. She walked lightly to the hearth and sat down by the fender. As she washed her paws and rearranged her damp fur, paying special attention to the ruff round her neck and to her bedraggled tail, the old man noticed that she was not the half-starved bag of bones he had thought. Her fur was thick and soft and her whiskers fierce and majestic. Even her tail now fluffed out to twice its previous size.

The fire was a small one as wood was hard to get in bad weather. When the cat had finished washing herself she began to shiver. Her whole body shook and her pointed teeth chattered. She crouched as near to the fire as she could get.

'You're in a bad way, pussy,' said the old man, whose own hands were stiff and blue with cold. 'I'll throw on another log.'

As the flames leapt and danced, the cat stopped shivering. She lay on her side and warmed her front. Then she rolled over and warmed her back. She waved her paws and lazily flapped her tail. Her mouth appeared to smile and from her throat came a deep, rich purr.

The old man was delighted. The flames crackled and the clock ticked and the visitor purred. How cosy he felt, and how peaceful and how contented! He quite forgot how hungry he was.

When the log was burned away and the flames died down the cat began to shiver again, and the chattering of her teeth was as loud as the ticking of the clock. The old man fetched the last two logs in the box, and soon the deep, rich purring began. They sat together, enjoying the glowing warmth.

It was after midnight when the old man went to bed, tucking the blankets snugly round himself and trying not to think of the empty cupboard. He thought of his visitor instead. Why, she might have starved to death if he hadn't given her a good meal.

Presently he felt something land on his bed and saw two green eyes shining. The cat wriggled her way under the bed-clothes and settled herself against his chest. She purred and marked time with her front paws as cats do when they are sleepy and happy. The old man had been feeling chilly, even under the blankets, but once the cat had got comfortably settled he felt a warmth creeping through him, from top to toe, and he soon fell into a deep sleep.

Next morning, the two of them woke late. The wind had dropped and the sun was shining on a light powdering of snow. There was nothing in the house to eat, so there was no breakfast to get ready, and no more wood, so there was no fire to light.

The cat ran to the door and lifted her paw and mewed gently, asking to be let out. The old man opened the door and she stepped out into the sunshine.

'You don't look like the same cat,' he said. 'You seem fatter. You hold your head as proudly as if you were a queen. Your fur shines and your eyes are like jewels.'

He had never before heard a cat speak, but he was not surprised when she looked back over her shoulder and said clearly:

'I have drunk your milk and eaten your bread and finished your meat and used up your last logs. Why don't you drive me away and slam the door?'

'Drive you away! Slam the door!' repeated the old man, in a puzzled voice. 'Why should I do that? You were cold and wet and hungry. Now you are warm and dry and satisfied. We were strangers, you and I. Now we are friends.' He bent down and stroked her furry back.

'Goodbye, my friend, goodbye!'

She ran along the path, jumped over the wall, and disappeared among the trees. It was some time later that the old man realized she had left no foot-prints in the powdery snow.

The cottage seemed empty and lonely, so he decided to tidy it up and occupy his mind with other things. He opened the cupboard and took out the empty milk jug to wash it. But it felt strangely heavy. It was empty no longer, filled to the brim with rich, creamy milk. The plate, too, was no longer bare. A thick, tempting mutton chop lay on it. Nearby was a loaf of bread, crisply baked and smelling delicious. The log box, standing in the corner, was piled high with logs of various sizes.

Soon the fire was blazing, the meat sizzling in the pan, and a bowl of bread and milk standing in the hearth. That night, when the old man went to bed and pulled up the blankets, the same warmth crept from head to foot, lulling him to sleep.

For the rest of his life, the cupboard always contained food and there were logs in the corner. The black cat never came again though sometimes, when the old man sat nodding by the fire, he heard not only the crackling of the fire and the ticking of the clock, but the deep purring of his friend.

This story is by Ruth Ainsworth.

Ignatius Binz and his Magnificent Nose

Now, there are two things you should know about Ignatius Binz: one is that he was born on top of a perfume factory, and the other is that he had a magnificent nose.

Not that his nose was particularly pretty, being small and freckled and snubbed, much like any other nose. It was what this nose could *do* that was extraordinary.

Ignatius had not been in the world for very long before his mother noticed something unusual; her son smiled when she made spicy sauces. He spat out his dummy and his nose sniffed happily as the fragrance of rich foods drifted up. By the time he could crawl, Ignatius could tell you in one sniff exactly what was cooking for dinner. And on his mother's birthday he created a new sauce so delicious that tears came to the family's eyes.

'The boy has inherited his grandfather's nose!' Mrs Binz cried. 'With him in the business, our factory will be great again. Everyone will want perfume by Binz.'

Mrs Binz didn't believe in wasting time. As soon as Ignatius could walk, she took him on a tour of the Binz Perfume Factory. He liked putting his nose

into the little test-tubes, all neatly labelled and smelling of spice and blossom. But most interesting were those bottles of woody, crisp smells that came from mosses and ferns. There were little pictures on these bottles, of forests with rain-shiny leaves, and trees that grew as high as you could see. Ignatius would have liked to visit these places, but his father told him not to be silly.

'Perfume, my boy, that's your calling. Why bother to *go* to a place when you can smell it in a bottle? Ignatius Binz, the world is at the end of your nose.'

Ignatius looked down at the floor of the perfume factory and thought the world must be a rather flat kind of place, but he didn't say anything more about travelling.

As Ignatius grew, so did the remarkable powers of his nose. Blindfolded, he could tell you the name of any scent. In a finger-snap he could make a fragrance of his own. Now Ignatius spent all his time downstairs at the factory. He wore a white coat and sat in a clean windowless office. Stacked on shelves around him were bottles of chemicals starting with B, and books about the History of Perfume. But all Ignatius really needed was his nose.

His nose told him many things: which smells

were the most delicious, and how much more delicious they would be if he added, say, just a hint of wood pine.

Now Ignatius was inventing perfumes no-one had ever imagined. His perfumes made people dream of impossible things: flowers in the snow, starlight at noon, desert roses. His perfumes shocked, startled, *sang*. Mr Binz called them 'Desert Ice' and 'Moroccan Moon', and they sold very well.

But alone in his room at night, Ignatius wondered if there mightn't be more to life than perfume. It wasn't very exciting, he thought, to sit in an office with a lot of test tubes. And was it, Ignatius wondered deep in his soul, very useful?

Ignatius longed for Adventure, Travel and Danger. He saw himself saving lives, rescuing people from explosions and certain death. He wanted to see the world!

But his mother only patted his head. 'Your fortune, Ignatius Binz, is in your nose. And you don't have to go far to find that!'

One day, as Ignatius bent over a fresh tub of gardenias, he saw something moving under the petals. Reaching in, he lifted the creature up on his finger. A tiny golden spider, no bigger than a bud, crawled into his palm and waved at him.

'Hello,' said Ignatius.

'How do you do?' said the spider.

From that moment, Ignatius was best friends with Aristan. (Yes, that was the spider's name.) While Ignatius mixed rose and jasmine petals and sniffed his test-tubes, Aristan kept him company. Swinging gently from a strand of his web, he told Ignatius about the world beyond the factory – about forests with rain-shiny leaves that grow as high as you can see.

'I would like to visit those places,' Ignatius said.

'You can!' replied Aristan. 'Your nose is very special, but it is made for more than perfumes. Saving lives could be your destiny! Just think, you could smell danger before anyone. Find it and remember it – the smell of danger.'

With Aristan's words in his ear, and a suitcase in his hand, Ignatius set off to see the world. He walked through jungles steaming in the sun. He smelled fresh cut grass and the salt of the ocean. Sometimes, he camped under trees that grew as high as he could see. 'Having a lovely time,' he wrote to his parents, as he ate marshmallows in the moonlight.

One afternoon, when he'd reached the out-skirts of a city, a strange smell tickled his nose. It was sharp, peppery, smouldering. 'Aha!' thought

Ignatius, 'at last! *This* is the smell of danger.'

He sniffed. His nose told him the burning was far away, but the smell hung like an echo on the air, pulling him toward it.

Now he began to run, and as he ran, night fell, furring the streets with darkness. Deeper and deeper into the city he ran, following his nose through winding alleys and around shadowy corners until the smell of burning became so strong that he knew he had arrived.

'BOTTLED GAS FACTORY', the sign said on the building in front of him. And in smaller letters, 'Danger – keep out'.

Ignatius shivered. He knew about gas and fire from working at the perfume factory. If a flame just breathed on those bottles of gas, an explosion like a volcano would erupt.

He crept round the outside of the building and peered into the windows. The great, dark rooms were full of pipes and machinery. There was no-one about; just the dark and the smell of danger. And then he saw it.

In a small room at the back of the factory a pile of rags lay smouldering. Even as he watched, a spark kindled, and a red glow, as fierce as sunset, lit up the room. It showed him books and files and boxes of paper, and flames now danced angrily between them. He gasped as the flames joined and swelled until they almost reached the ceiling. At any moment the whole factory could go up.

Ignatius hurtled back down the path – up the hill, along the street, past the darkened doorways. He found a phone box and dialled Emergency.

'The Fire Brigade, please, to the Bottled Gas Factory,' he said. 'And step on it!'

When the big red fire engines came roaring down the street, Ignatius was ready for them.

'Follow me!' he cried, and ten, twenty, thirty men – in blue uniforms with shiny buttons – leaped out and ran after him.

Ignatius led them around to the room at the back, just in time to see the flames shatter the glass of its windows. He watched as the men shouted orders to each other, hauling out hoses as fat as pythons.

'Water on!' they shouted, and, 'Ten metres to the left!'

Ignatius thought his heart would burst with pride as the jets of water shot over the flames.

The next day, back at the perfume factory, Mr and Mrs Binz were having their breakfast. Mr Binz gave a start of surprise when he spotted his son on the front page of the newspaper.

'Small boy saves city,' he read aloud to his wife.

'Hmm?' she said, sipping her tea.

'The magnificent nose of Ignatius Binz led him to a fire,' read on Mr Binz, 'that could have destroyed the city of Springstep. The Mayor of Springstep said yesterday, "Ignatius Binz is the kind of man we need in this town."'

'Fancy that!' said Mr Binz, putting down the paper.

'He was born with his grandfather's nose,' said Mrs Binz fondly.

That day, Mr and Mrs Binz went to Springstep. They found their son at the top of a tall tower, overlooking the Springstep Forest. With him was a band of men in blue uniforms and shiny buttons, enjoying their lunch and the splendid view.

After the Binzs had met everyone (and eaten lasagne with spicy sauce), Ignatius took them through to his office. 'IGNATIUS BINZ', the sign said on the door, 'CAPTAIN, FIRE BRIGADE'.

Ignatius showed them a desk with nine tele-

phones and a map of the world on the wall. 'I get to travel a lot,' Ignatius told his parents, after they had hugged and kissed and congratulated him. 'Way up here on the tower I can sniff out trouble before it gets started. I deal in fires, floods and any number of Natural Disasters.'

Now Mr and Mrs Binz often left the perfume factory to visit their son, but they didn't always find him at home. For the magnificent nose of Ignatius Binz led him to many different parts of the world: wherever the smell of danger called him.

This story is by Anna Fienberg.

The Faces of the Czar

The cupboard in my grandmother's bedroom was big and brown, with a long mirror set into its central panel. If you opened the cupboard doors, there were shelves upon shelves filled with sheets and pillowcases, towels and tablecloths, and even some containing folded underwear and lots of rolled-up brown balls of stockings. Right at the bottom there was a drawer, and it was in this drawer that the button-box was kept. It was made of tin: a dull, silvery colour. I don't know what used to be kept in it, nor what it had held when it first came into the house; but now it was full of buttons. When I took it out of the drawer and moved it around in my hands, all the buttons made a sushy-rattly sound as they moved against the metal sides of the box. I liked spilling them on to the black and yellow tiles of the bedroom floor, where I arranged them in groups according to size, or colour, or beauty, or spread them out in huge patterns all around me. Sometimes, my cousins and I used the buttons as pretend money. Silver ones were the most valuable of all, and there were six buttons (from a dress that had once belonged to my aunt in America) which had the face of a man with a beard and a crown scratched on to them.

'Such a face,' my grandmother said, 'could only belong to a Czar. Do you know what a Czar was?'

I shook my head.

'A Czar was a Russian emperor, the kind of ruler whose very lightest word was law, the kind of ruler before whom everyone trembled, and more especially the poor peasant, trying to scratch a bare living out of a tiny patch of ground. And of course, as well as being powerful, and wicked more often than not, Czars, like all other rulers, were in the habit of having little pictures of themselves stamped on to every coin in the kingdom. All this talk of Czars reminds me of the story of Frankel the farmer. Have I told you about him before?'

'No, never,' I said. 'Tell me about him now.'

'So put all the buttons back in the box and I'll begin.

'Are they all in? Good. Now, long ago, in a very far away and neglected corner of Russia, about a day's ride from the Czar's Summer Palace, there lived a farmer called Frankel. On this particular day that I'm telling you of, Frankel was happily occupied digging up turnips in what he called his field, but which in truth was a piece of land about the size of a tablecloth. He was content. The sun was shining for once, the turnips had all turned out well, large and pleasantly mauve and white in colour, and their leaves were so prettily green and feathery that Frankel sang as he worked. He was absorbed in his labours, so that he hardly noticed the horseman drawing nearer and nearer, until the noise of the hoof-beats on the dry earth of the road made him look up. What he saw made him drop his spade in amazement. It was the Czar. Frankel bowed deeply.

"Do not be surprised, my friend," said the Czar. "Often, when I'm sick to death of court councils and endless feasts, I saddle my horse and go riding about my kingdom, talking to my subjects. I am very interested to observe that although the hair on your head is grey, the hairs of your beard are still black. It's something I've often noticed in people

before, and yet no-one seems to know the reason for it."

"O, mighty Czar," Frankel replied (reasoning that he couldn't possibly be too polite to a Czar), "I am only a poor Jewish farmer, but the reason is this. The hairs on my head started growing when I was born. Those on my chin only started growing when I was thirteen years old, after the Bar Mitzvah ceremony at which I became a man. Therefore, the hairs on my chin are much younger and not yet grey."

"Amazing!" said the Czar. "How simple and yet how logical! I'm overjoyed to have discovered the answer to a question that has long been puzzling me. Now, I beg of you, my friend, tell no-one else what you have told me. Let it remain a secret between us. Do you agree?"

"I will only reveal our secret after I have seen your face a hundred times, Sire," said Frankel. So the Czar set off on his horse, chuckling to himself, and Frankel continued digging up his turnips.

When the Czar arrived at the Palace, he asked all his advisers to gather round.

"Here," he said, "is a question. Why does the hair on the head grow grey before the hair of the beard? Whoever can answer that question for me will be promoted to the position of Chief

Adviser to the Czar, and will sit in a specially-fashioned silver throne studded with lumps of amber the size of small onions."

All the advisers scurried about, asking everyone they met, consulting books too heavy to be carried, and working out every possibility on scrolls of paper a yard long. This went on for weeks. Finally, two of the chancellors discussed the matter.

"I remember," said one, "that on the day the Czar asked us the question, he had come back from a ride to the Western Territory. Perhaps he found the answer there. If we ride in the same direction, maybe we'll come across it too."

Thus it happened that one rainy day as Frankel was listening sadly to the sucking noises made by his boots entering and leaving the mud, two horsemen galloped up to where he was standing.

"Good day to you, farmer," said one of the horsemen. "We are advisers to the Czar, and we have reason to think that the Czar may have ridden this way a few weeks ago."

"He did," Frankel agreed. "And now, here you are. This part of the world hasn't ever been quite so busy. A person hardly has the leisure to tend his property."

"But did you tell the Czar why it is that the hair on the head turns grey before the hair of the beard?"

"I did, but I'm not at liberty to tell you gentlemen."

The chancellors sighed. "Is there nothing we can do to persuade you to change your mind?"

Frankel considered. "One hundred silver roubles will change my mind instantly."

"Then take these, my friend," said one of the chancellors, "and tell us the answer to the riddle."

Frankel took the coins, sat down in the road, and spread the coins out on his lap to count them. When he had finished, he told the Czar's advisers exactly what he had told the Czar. The men sprang into their saddles and left for the Palace at a gallop, feeling very pleased with themselves, but not as pleased as Frankel, who had suddenly acquired wealth.

The trouble only began when they came to the Czar and told him the answer.

"How can you possibly know this?" shouted the Czar.

"We met a Jewish farmer called Frankel on the road," they said, "and he told us."

"And he undertook to say nothing, the scoundrel!" The Czar stamped his foot and sent for his Chief of Police. "Go to the farm of the Jew, Frankel, and bring him here at once. Also, alert the firing squad. This will be Frankel's last day on earth."

Well, eventually the police brought Frankel to see the Czar.

"What have you to say for yourself, you wretch?" yelled the Czar. "Did you not promise me that you would not reveal the secret you told me?"

"I said," Frankel whispered, "that I would only reveal it after I had seen your face a hundred times."

"But this is only the second time you have seen me, you worm! What have you to say for yourself before I have you shot?"

"Forgive me, Czar," said Frankel, and he took out the bag containing the hundred silver roubles

which the chancellors had given him. "Here are one hundred coins. I have looked at every one. Therefore, I'm sure you will agree, I have seen your face one hundred times."

The Czar was stunned, full of admiration for Frankel's sharp wits.

"I shall get rid of all my advisers and appoint you instead," he chuckled. "You shall sit at my left hand on a silver throne studded with amber lumps the size of small onions. You shall want for nothing, my friend."

And so Frankel lived to a ripe old age, and became the richest and most powerful man in Russia, next only to the Czar himself.'

This story is by Adèle Geras.

A Day When Frogs Wear Shoes

My little brother Huey, my best friend Gloria and I were sitting on our front steps. It was one of those hot summer days when everything stands still. We didn't know what to do. We were watching the grass grow. It didn't grow fast.

'You know something?' Gloria said. 'This is a slow day.'

'It's so slow the dogs don't bark,' Huey said.

'It's so slow the flies don't fly,' Gloria said.

'It's so slow ice cream wouldn't melt,' I said.

'If we had any ice cream,' Huey said.

'But we haven't,' Gloria said.

We watched the grass some more.

'We'd better do something,' I said.

'Like what?' Gloria asked.

'We could visit Dad,' Huey said.

'That's a *terrible* idea,' I said.

My father has a workshop about a mile from our house, where he fixes cars. Usually it is fun to visit him. If he has customers, he always introduces us as if we were important guests. If he doesn't have company, sometimes he lets us ride in the cars he puts up on the lift. Sometimes he buys us treats.

'Huey,' I said, 'usually, visiting Dad is a good idea. Today, it's a dangerous idea.'

'Why?' Gloria said.

'Because we're bored,' I said. 'My dad hates it when people are bored. He says the world is so interesting nobody should ever be bored.'

'I see,' Gloria said, as if she didn't.

'So we'll go to see him,' Huey said, 'and we just won't tell him we're bored. We're bored, but we won't tell him.'

'Just you remember that!' I said.

'Oh, I'll remember,' Huey said.

Huey was wearing his angel look. When he has that look, you know he'll never remember anything.

Huey and I put on sweat bands. Gloria put on dark glasses. We started out.

The sun shone up at us from the pavements. Even the shadows on the street were hot as blankets.

Huey picked up a stick and scratched it along the pavement. 'Oh, we're bored,' he muttered. 'Bored, bored, bored, bored!'

'Huey!' I yelled. I wasn't bored any more. I was nervous.

Finally we reached a sign:

RALPH'S CAR HOSPITAL
Punctures
Rust
Dents & Bashes
Bad Brakes
Bad Breaks
Unusual Complaints

That's my dad's sign. My dad is Ralph.

The car park had three cars in it. Dad was inside the workshop, lifting the bonnet of another car. He didn't have any customers with him, so we didn't get to shake hands and feel like visiting mayors or V.I.P.s.

'Hi, Dad,' I said.

'Hi!' my dad said.

'We're—'

I didn't trust Huey. I stepped on his foot.

'We're on a hike,' I said.

'Well, nice of you to stop by,' my father said. 'If you want, you can stay a while and help me.'

'OK,' we said.

So Huey sorted nuts and bolts. Gloria shined bumpers with a rag. I held a new windscreen wiper while my dad put it on a car window.

'Nice work, Huey and Julian and Gloria!' my dad said when we had finished.

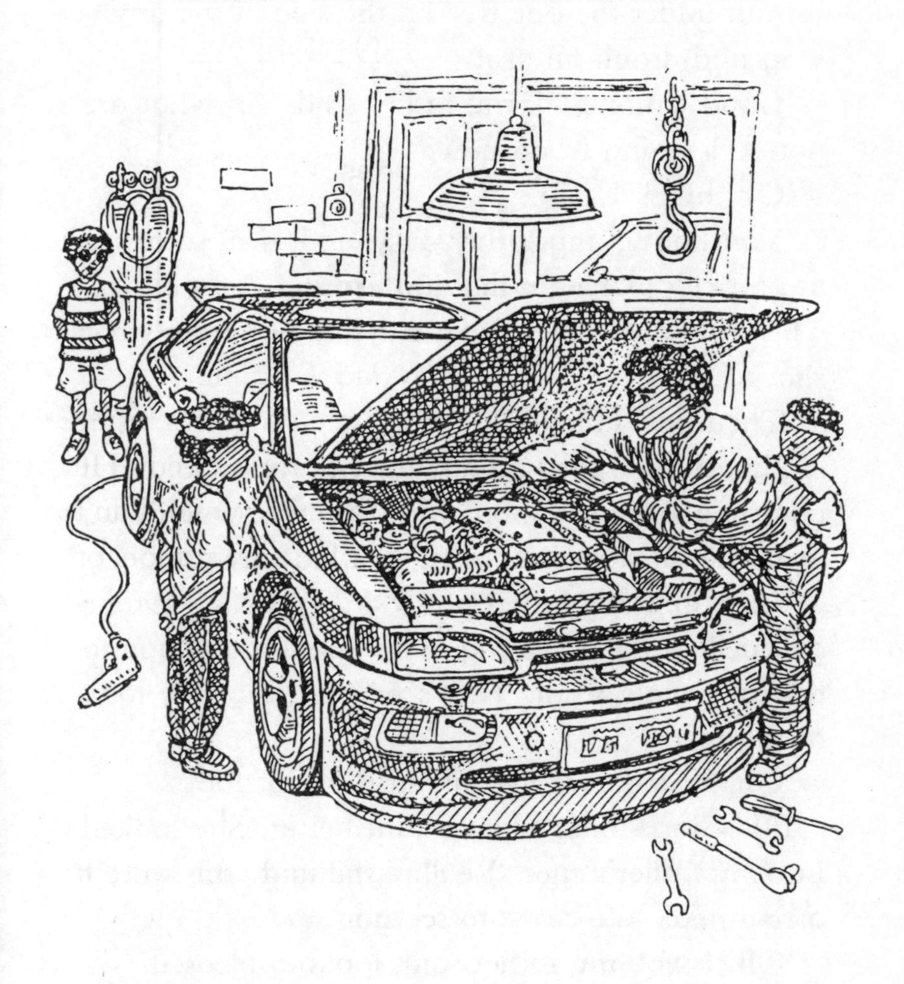

And then he sent us to the shop across the street to buy paper cups and ice cubes and a can of frozen lemonade.

We mixed the lemonade in the shop. Then we

sat out under the one tree by the side of the drive-way and drank all of it.

'Good lemonade!' my father said. 'So what are you kids going to do now?'

'Oh, hike!' I said.

'You know,' my father answered, 'I'm surprised at you kids picking a hot day like today for a hike. The ground is so hot. On a day like this, frogs wear shoes!'

'They do?' Huey said.

'Especially if they go hiking,' my father said. 'Of course, a lot of frogs, on a day like this, would stay at home. So I wonder why you kids are hiking.'

Sometimes my father notices too much. Then he gets yellow lights shining in his eyes, asking you to tell the whole truth. That's when I know to look at my feet.

'Oh,' I said, 'we *like* hiking.'

But Gloria didn't know any better. She looked into my father's eyes. 'Really,' she said, 'this wasn't a real hike. We came to see you.'

'Oh, I see!' my father said, looking pleased.

'Because we were bored,' Huey said.

My father jumped up so fast he tipped over his lemonade cup. 'BORED!' my father yelled. 'You were BORED?'

He picked up his cup and waved it in the air.

'And you think *I* don't get BORED?' my father roared, sprinkling out a few last drops of lemonade from his cup. 'You think I don't get bored fixing cars when it's so hot that frogs wear shoes?'

'"This is such an interesting world that nobody should ever be bored." That's what you said,' I reminded him.

'Last week,' Huey added.

'Ummm,' my father said. He went quiet.

He rubbed his hand over his mouth, the way he does when he's thinking.

'Why, of course,' my father said, 'I remember that. And it's the perfect, absolute truth. People absolutely SHOULD NOT get bored! However—' He paused. 'It just happens that, sometimes, they do.'

My father rubbed a line in the dirt with his shoe. He was thinking so hard I could see his thoughts standing by the tree and sitting on all the bumpers of the cars.

'You know, if you three would kindly help me some more, I could leave half an hour early, and we could drive down by the river.'

'We'll help,' I said.

'Yes, and then we can look for frogs!' Huey said.

So we stayed. We learned how to make an indicator light blink. And afterwards, on the way to the river, my dad bought us all ice cream cones. The ice cream did melt. Huey's melted all down the front of his shirt. It took ten paper napkins and the river to clean him up.

After Huey's shirt was clean, we took our shoes and socks off and went paddling.

We looked for special rocks under the water – the ones that are beautiful until you take them out of the water, when they get dry and not so bright.

We found skipping stones and tried to see who could get the most skips from a stone.

We saw a school of minnows going as fast as they could get away from us.

But we didn't see any frogs.

'If you want to see frogs,' my father said, 'you'll have to walk further down the bank and look hard.'

So we decided to do that.

'Fine!' my father said. 'But I'll stay here. I think I'm ready for a little nap.'

'Naps are boring!' we said.

'Sometimes it's nice to be bored,' my father said.

We left him with his eyes closed, sitting under a tree.

Huey saw the first frog. He almost stepped on it. It jumped into the water, and we ran after it.

Huey caught it and picked it up, and then I saw

another one. I grabbed it.

It was slippery and strong and its body was cold, just like it wasn't the middle of summer.

Then Gloria caught one too. The frogs wriggled in our hands, and we felt their hearts beating. Huey looked at their funny webbed feet.

'Their feet are good for swimming,' he said, 'but Dad is wrong. They don't wear shoes!'

'No,' Gloria said. 'They never wear shoes.'

'Let's go and tell him,' I said.

We threw our frogs back into the river. They made little trails swimming away from us. And then we went back to my father.

He was sitting under the tree with his eyes shut. It looked as if he hadn't moved an inch.

'We found frogs,' Huey said, 'and we've got news for you. They don't wear shoes!'

My father's eyes opened. 'They don't?' he said. 'Well, I can't be right about everything. Dry your feet. Put your shoes on. It's time to go.'

We all sat down to put on our shoes.

I pulled out a sock and put it on.

I stuck my foot into my shoe. My foot wouldn't go in.

I picked up the shoes and looked inside.

'Oh no!' I yelled.

There were two little eyes inside my shoe,

looking out at me. Huey and Gloria grabbed their socks. All our shoes had frogs in them, every one.

'What did I tell you,' my father said.

'You were right,' we said. 'It's a day when frogs wear shoes!'

This story is by Ann Cameron.

The Cost of Night

There was once a king called Merrion the Carefree who was inclined to be foolish. Perhaps this was because his wife had died when her baby daughter was born some years before, and so there was no-one to keep an eye on the king. His worst failing was that he could never resist a game of chance; but of course all his subjects knew about this, and none of them would have dreamed of suggesting a game.

However it happened once that the king was returning home after a visit to a distant province of his kingdom. Towards twilight he came to a great river that was swift-flowing and wide. As he

hesitated on the brink, for he was but an indifferent swimmer, he saw, moving through the reeds, an enormously large crocodile, with teeth as big as tenpins, cold expressionless yellow eyes, and a skin that looked as old and wrinkled and horny as the world itself.

'Ho, crocodile!' said King Merrion. 'I am your lord and ruler, Merrion the Carefree, so it is plainly your duty to turn crossways over the river and make a bridge, in order that I may walk dry-shod from bank to bank.'

At this the crocodile gave a great guttural choking bark, which might have been either a sardonic laugh or a respectful cough.

'Ahem, Your Majesty! I am no subject of yours, being indeed a traveller like yourself, but out of courtesy and good fellowship I don't mind making a bridge across the river for you, on one condition: that you play a game of heads or tails with me.'

Now at this point, of course, the king should have had the sense to draw back. Better if he had slept all night on the bank, or travelled upstream till he came to the next bridge, however far off it lay. But he was tired, and eager to be home; besides, at the notion of a game, all sense and caution fled out of his head.

'I'll be glad to play with you, crocodile,' he said. 'But only one quick game, mind, for I am already late and should have been home hours ago.'

So the crocodile, smiling all the way along his hundred teeth, turned sideways-on, and King Merrion walked on his horny back dry-shod from one river-bank to the other. Although the crocodile's back was covered in mud it was not slippery because of all the wrinkles.

When the king had stepped right over the hundred-tooth smile, and off the crocodile's long muddy snout, he looked about him and picked up a flat stone which was white on one side and brown on the other.

'This will do for our game, if you agree,' he said.

'Certainly I agree,' said the crocodile, smiling more than ever.

'What shall we play for?'

'The loser must grant the winner any gift he asks. You may throw first,' the crocodile said politely.

So the king threw, and the crocodile snapped, 'White!' Sure enough, the stone landed white side up.

Then the crocodile threw, and the king called, 'Brown!' But again the stone landed white side up.

Then the king threw, and again the crocodile said 'White!' and the stone landed white side up. For the fact of the matter was that the crocodile was not a genuine crocodile at all, but a powerful enchanter who chose to appear in that shape.

So the crocodile guessed right every time, and the king guessed wrong, until he was obliged to acknowledge that he had lost the game.

'What do you want for your gift?' said he.

The crocodile smiled hugely, until he looked like a tunnel through the Rocky Mountains.

'Give me,' he said, 'all the dark in your kingdom.'

At this the king was most upset. 'I am not sure

that the dark is mine to give away,' he said. 'I would rather that you had asked me for all the gold in my treasury.'

'What use is gold to me?' said the crocodile. 'Remember your kingly word. The dark I want, and the dark I must have.'

'Oh, very well,' said the king, biting his lip. 'If you must, you must.'

So the crocodile opened his toothy mouth even wider, and sucked, with a suction stronger than the widest whirlpool, and all the dark in King Merrion's kingdom came rushing along and was sucked down his great cavernous throat. Indeed he sucked so hard that he swallowed up, not only the dark that covered King Merrion's country, but the dark that lay over the entire half of the world facing away from the sun, just as you might suck the pulp off a ripe plum. And he smacked his lips over it, for dark was his favourite food.

'That was delicious!' he said. 'Many thanks, Majesty! May your shadow never grow less!'

And with another loud harsh muddy laugh he disappeared.

King Merrion went home to his palace, where he found everyone in the greatest dismay and astonishment. For instead of there being night, as would have been proper at that time, the whole country was bathed in a strange unearthly light, clear as day, but a day in which nothing cast any shadow. Flowers which had shut their petals opened them again, birds peevishly brought their heads out from under their wings, owls and bats, much puzzled, returned to their thickets, and the little princess Gudrun refused to go to bed.

Indeed, after a few days, the unhappy king realized that he had brought a dreadful trouble to his kingdom – and to the whole world – by his rash promise. Without a regular spell of dark every twelve hours, nothing went right – plants grew tall and weak and spindly, cattle and poultry became confused and stopped producing milk and eggs, winds gave up blowing, and the weather went all to pieces. As for people, they were soon in a worse muddle than the cows and hens. At first everybody tried to work all night, so as to make the most of this extra daylight, but they soon became cross and exhausted and longed for rest. However it was almost impossible to sleep, for no matter what they did, covering their windows with thick curtains, shutting their doors, hiding under the bedclothes and bandaging their eyes, not a scrap of dark could anybody find. The crocodile had swallowed it all.

As for the children, they ran wild. Bed-time had ceased to exist.

The little princess Gudrun was the first to become tired of such a state of affairs. She was very fond of listening to stories, and what she enjoyed almost more than anything else was to lie in bed with her eyes tight shut in the warm dark, and remember the fairy-tales that her nurse used to tell her. But in the hateful daylight that went on and on it was not possible to do this. So she went to confide in her greatest friend and ask his service.

Gudrun's greatest friend was a great black horse called Houniman, a battle-charger who had been sent as a gift to King Merrion several years before; battles were not very frequent at that time, so Houniman mostly roamed, grazing the palace meadows. Now Gudrun sought him out, and gave him a handful of golden corn, and tried to pretend, by burying her face in his long, thick, black mane, that the dark had come again.

'What shall we do about it, Houniman?' she said.

'It is obviously no use expecting your silly father to put matters right,' Houniman replied.

'No, I am afraid you are right,' Gudrun said, sighing.

'So, as he has given away all the dark in the entire world, we shall have to find out where dark comes from and how we can get some more of it.'

'But who,' she said, 'would know such a thing?'

Houniman considered. 'If we travel towards Winter,' he said at length, 'perhaps we might learn something, for in winter the dark grows until it almost swallows up the light.'

'Good,' said the princess, 'let us travel towards Winter.' So she fetched a woolly cloak, and filled her pockets with bread-and-cheese, and brought a bag of corn for Houniman, and they started out. Nobody noticed them go, since all the people in the kingdom were in such a state of muddle and upset, and King Merrion worst of all.

The princess rode on Houniman and he galloped steadily northwards for seven days and what ought to have been seven nights, over a sea of ice, until they came to the Land of Everlasting Winter, where the words freeze as you speak them, and even thoughts rattle in your head like icicles.

There they found the Lord of Winter, in the form of a great eagle, brooding on a rock.

'Sir,' called Gudrun from a good way off – for it was so cold in his neighbourhood that the very birds froze in the air and hung motionless – 'can you tell us where we can find a bit of dark?'

He lifted his head with its great hooked beak and gave them an angry look.

'Why should I help you? I have only one little

piece of dark, and I am keeping it for myself, under my wing, so that it may grow.'

'Does dark grow?' said Gudrun.

'Of course it grows, stupid girl! Cark! Be off with you!' And the eagle spread one wing (keeping the other tight folded) so that a great white flurry of snow and wind drove towards Gudrun and Houniman, and they turned and galloped away.

At the edge of the Land of Winter they saw an old woman leading a reindeer loaded with wood.

'Mother,' called Gudrun, 'can you tell us where we might find a bit of dark?'

'Give me a piece of bread-and-cheese for myself and some corn for my beast and I will consider.'

So they gave her the bread and corn and she considered. Presently she said,

'There will be plenty of dark in the past. You should go to No Man's Land, the frontier where the present slips into the past, and perhaps you might be able to pick up a bit of dark there.'

'Good,' said the princess, 'that sounds hopeful. But in which direction does the past lie?'

'Towards the setting sun, of course!' snapped the old woman, and she gave her reindeer a thump to make it jog along faster.

So Gudrun and Houniman turned towards the setting sun and galloped on for seven days and what should have been seven nights, until they reached No Man's Land. This was a strange and misty region, with low hills and marshes; in the middle of it they came to a great lake, on the shore of which sat an old poet in a little garden of cranberry shrubs. Instead of water the lake was filled with blue-grey mist, and the old poet was drawing out the mist in long threads, and twisting them and turning them into poems. It was very silent all around there, with not a living creature, and the old poet was so absorbed in what he did that he never lifted his head until they stood beside him.

'Can you tell us, uncle poet,' said Gudrun, 'where we might pick up a bit of dark?'

'Dark?' he said absently. 'Eh, what's that? You want a bit of dark? There's plenty at the bottom of the lake.'

So Gudrun dismounted and walked to the edge of the lake, and looked down through the mist. Thicker and thicker it grew, darker and darker, down in the depths of the lake, and as she looked down she could see all manner of strange shapes, and some that seemed familiar too – faces that she had once known, places that she had once visited, all sunk down in the dark depths of the past. As she leaned over, the mist seemed to rise up around her, so that she began to become sleepy, to forget who she was and what she had come for . . .

'Gudrun! Come back!' cried Houniman loudly, and he stretched out his long neck and caught hold of her by the hair and pulled her back, just as she was about to topple into the lake.

'Climb on my back and let's get out of here!' he said. 'Dark or no dark, this place is too dangerous!'

But Gudrun cried to the poet, 'Uncle poet, isn't there any other place where we might pick up a bit of dark?'

'Dark?' he said. 'You want a bit of dark? Well,

I suppose you might try the Gates of Death; dark grows around there.'

'Where are the Gates of Death?'

'You must go to the middle of the earth, where the sky hangs so low that it is resting on the ground, and the rivers run uphill. There you will find the Gates of Death.'

And he went back to his poem-spinning.

So they galloped on for seven days and what should have been seven nights, until the mountains grew higher and higher, and the sky hung lower and lower, and at last they came to the Gates of Death.

This place was so frightening that Gudrun's heart went small inside her, because everything seemed to be turning into something else. The sky was dropping into the mountains, and the mountains piercing into the sky. A great river ran uphill, boiling, and in front of the Gates of Death themselves a huge serpent lay coiled, with one yellow eye half open, watching as they drew near.

'Cousin serpent,' called Gudrun, trying not to let her teeth chatter, 'can you tell us where we might pick up a little piece of dark?'

'Ssss! Look about you, stupid girl!' hissed the serpent.

When Gudrun looked about her she saw that the

ground was heaving and shuddering as if some great live creature were buried underneath, and there were cracks and holes in the rock, through which little tendrils of dark came leaking out.

But as fast as they appeared, the serpent snapped them off and gobbled them up.

Gudrun stretched out her hand to pick an uncurling frond of dark.

'Sssstop!' hissed the serpent, darting out his head till she drew back her hand in a fright. 'All this dark is mine! And since my brother the crocodile ate all the dark in the world I will not part with one sprig of it, unless you give me something in return.'

'But what can I give you?' said Gudrun, trembling.

'You can give me your black horse. He is the colour of night, he will do very well for a tasty bite. Give him to me and you may pick one sprig of dark.'

'No, no, I cannot give you Houniman,' cried Gudrun weeping. 'He belongs to my father, not to me, and besides, he is my friend! I could not let him suffer such a dreadful fate. Take me instead, and let Houniman carry the dark back to my father's kingdom.'

'*You* wouldn't do at all,' hissed the serpent. 'You have golden hair and blue eyes, you would give me indigestion. No, it must be the horse, or I will not part with any dark. But you must take off his golden shoes, or they will give me hiccups.'

And Houniman whispered to the princess, 'Do as the serpent says, for I have a notion that all will come right. But take care to keep my golden shoes.'

So Gudrun wiped the tears from her eyes and Houniman lifted each foot in turn while she pulled off his golden shoes. And she put them in her pockets while the serpent sucked with a great whistling noise and sucked in Houniman, mane, tail and all.

Then Gudrun picked one little sprig of dark and ran weeping away from the Gates of Death. She ran on until she was tired, and then she turned and looked back. What was her horror to see that the serpent had uncoiled himself and was coming swiftly after her. 'For,' he had thought to himself, 'I merely told her that she could *pick* one sprig in exchange for the horse, I did not say that she could carry it away. It would be a pity to waste a good sprig.' So he was coming over the rocky ground, faster than a horse could gallop.

Quick as thought, Gudrun took one of the gold horseshoes out of her pocket and flung it so that it fell over the serpent, pinning him to the rock. Twist and writhe as he might, he could not get free, and she was able to run on until he was left far behind.

She passed through No Man's Land, but she was careful not to go too near the lake of mist. And she passed through the Land of Everlasting Winter,

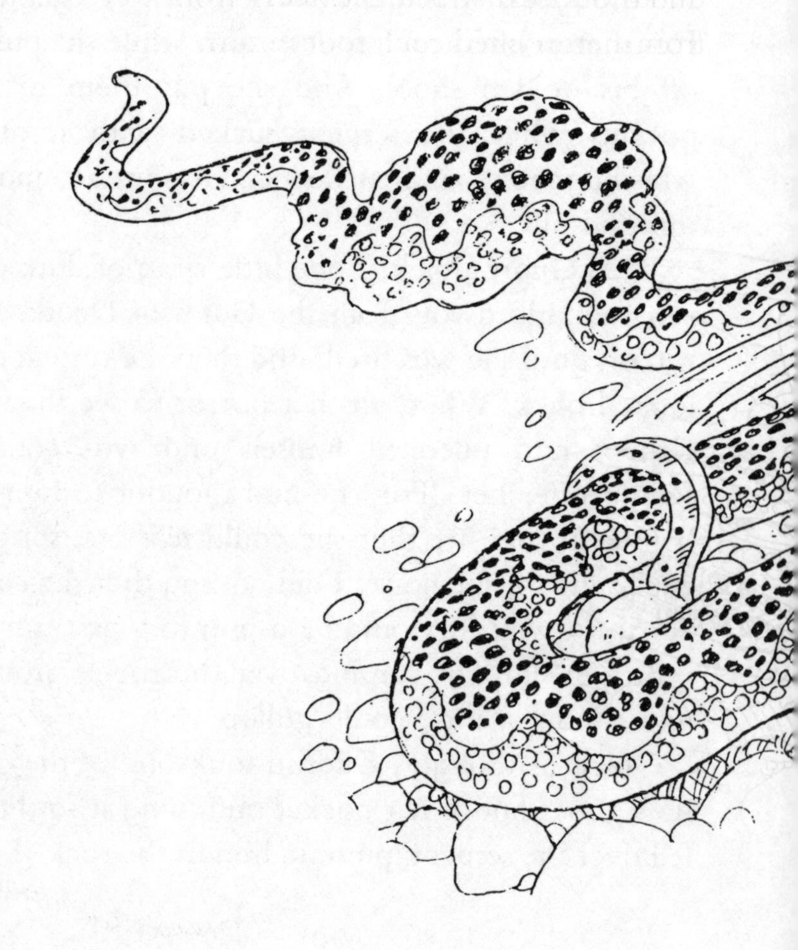

where the eagle sat guarding his little bit of dark. Then she came to the sea of ice, but now spring was coming, and the ice was beginning to melt.

'How shall I get over to the sea?' Gudrun wondered. 'Oh, how I wish my dear Houniman were here to advise me.'

But then she remembered the gold horseshoes and thought they might help. So she pulled another from her pocket, and directly she did so it spread

and stretched and turned into a boat. So Gudrun stepped into it, all the time hugging the little sprig of dark carefully against her heart, and the boat carried her safe across the sea.

Then she came to the borders of her father's kingdom, but it was still a long and weary way to his palace. For the journey that on Houniman's back had lasted only three times seven days and what should have been nights, took much longer on foot, and it was almost a year since she had left the Gates of Death. But the little sprig of dark had been growing and growing all the time.

Now Gudrun came to a wide, swift river.

In the reeds by the edge lay a crocodile, and he watched her approach with his yellow expressionless eyes.

'Ho there, little princess,' he said. 'I will play a game of heads or tails with you. If you win, I will turn my length across the river to make a bridge for you. And if I win, you shall give me the sprig of dark that you carry.'

But Gudrun did not share her father's fondness for games of chance.

'Thank you,' she said to the crocodile, 'but I have a bridge of my own.'

And she took out her third horseshoe, which immediately grew into a golden bridge, over which she crossed, leaving the crocodile to gnash his teeth with rage.

Gudrun ran on, slower and slower, for by now she was very tired, and the sprig of dark she carried had grown to the size of a young tree. But at last she reached her father's palace, and all the people ran out, with King Merrion in front, clapping their hands for joy.

'She has brought back the dark! Our darling princess has brought back the dark!'

'You must plant it in a safe, warm place and cherish it,' said Gudrun faintly. 'For I am afraid that the serpent and the crocodile may still come after it.'

So it was planted in the palace garden, and it slowly grew bigger and bigger – first as big as a nut tree, then big as a young birch, then big as a spreading oak. And King Merrion's subjects took turns to guard it, and Gudrun stayed beside it always.

But one day the envious crocodile came creeping along, in the shadow thrown by the tree of dark. The man set to guard the tree was almost asleep, for the shadow made him drowsy after so many months of daylight, but Gudrun saw the crocodile.

Quick as a flash she pulled out her fourth

horseshoe and threw it, pinning the crocodile to the ground.

But then she grew very anxious, 'For,' she said, 'what shall we do if the serpent comes? Now I have no more horseshoes! Oh, my dear, good, faithful friend Houniman, how I do miss you!'

And she laid her head against the trunk of the tree and wept bitter tears.

Now this watering was just what the tree needed, and that very minute it grew and flourished until its branches spread right across the sky and true night had come at last. Directly this happened, all the creatures of night who had stayed sulking in their hiding-places for so long, the owls and moths and night-herons, the bats, bitterns, nightjars and nightingales, and all the beasts of darkness, came out rejoicing and calling down blessings on the little princess Gudrun. But she still knelt weeping beside the tree.

Then the king of the night creatures, who was an enormous owl, looked down with his great eyes and saw the serpent creeping through the dark. (In the end, after many days, he had managed to wriggle out from under the horseshoe.)

'Thief, thief!' cried the owl. 'Kill him! Kill him!' And all the creatures of the dark flew down, pecking and tearing, until they had pecked the serpent into a thousand pieces. And out of the pieces sprang Houniman, alive and well!

Then Gudrun flung her arms round Houniman's neck and wept for joy, and King Merrion offered him any reward he cared to name for helping to bring back dark to the world.

'All I ask,' said Houniman, 'is that you set me free, for in my own land, far to the east, where night begins, I was king and lord over all the wild horses.'

'Willingly will I grant what you ask,' said King Merrion. So Houniman was given his freedom and he bade a loving farewell to the princess Gudrun and galloped away and away, home to his own country. But he sent back his son, the black colt Gandufer, to be the princess's lifelong companion and friend.

The creatures of night offered to peck the crocodile to pieces too, but King Merrion said no to that.

'I shall keep him a prisoner always, and the sight of him will be a reminder to me never again to get mixed up in a game of chance!' he said.

And so this was done.

This story is by Joan Aiken.

The Silly Ghosts Gruff

Once there were three ghosts. They were called the Silly Ghosts Gruff. There was Little Silly Ghost Gruff, Big Silly Ghost Gruff and Piddle-sized Silly Ghost Gruff. And they all lived in a field by a river. One day they thought they would like to cross the river to eat the grass on the other side.

Now, over this river there was a fridge, and underneath the fridge was a horrible roll. A horrible cheese roll.

So the Little Silly Ghost Gruff, he stepped on to the fridge, drip, drop, drip, drop, over the fridge; when suddenly, there on the fridge was the horrible roll. 'I'm a roll-fol-de-roll and you'll eat me for your supper!'

'Oh no, oh no, oh no,' said the Little Silly Ghost Gruff. 'I don't want to eat you. My big brother the Piddle-sized Silly Ghost Gruff is going to be coming along soon and he can eat you for his supper.'

‘Very well,’ said the horrible roll, ‘you can cross the fridge.’

And drip, drop, drip, drop, over the fridge went the Little Silly Ghost Gruff.

Next to come along was the Piddle-sized Silly Ghost Gruff.

Drip, drop, drip, drop, over the fridge he came until suddenly, there in front of him, on the fridge, was the horrible roll.

‘I’m a roll-fol-de-roll and you’ll eat me for your supper.’

‘Oh no, oh no, no, no,’ said the Piddle-sized Silly Ghost Gruff. ‘I don’t want to eat you. My big brother, the Big Silly Ghost Gruff is coming soon and he can eat you for his supper.’

‘Very well,’ said the roll, ‘you can cross the fridge.’

And drip, drop, drip, drop, the Piddle-sized Silly Ghost Gruff crossed the fridge to the other side.

Then along comes the Big Silly Ghost Gruff. Drip, drop, drip, drop, over the fridge and, suddenly, there was the horrible roll again.

‘I’m a roll-fol-de-roll and you’ll eat me for your supper.’

‘Oh can I? Oh can I?’ said the Big Silly Ghost Gruff.

And at that he ran at the horrible roll and went

straight through it (he was a ghost, don't forget).

And so over the fridge he went drip, drop, drip, drop, till he got to the other side.

And from that day on, no roll, no cheese roll, or ham roll or even a jam roll ever bothered the Silly Ghosts Gruff ever again.

This story is by Michael Rosen.

Esben and the Witch

Once upon a time there was a man who had twelve sons. Eleven of these sons were big, lusty lads; but the twelfth, whose name was Esben, was only a little fellow. The eleven elder brothers despised Esben, and his father thought nothing of him. It was only Esben's mother who had a soft corner for him in her heart. So Esben mostly stayed at home amd helped his mother, whilst his eleven brothers worked with their father in the fields.

Now when these eleven sons were grown to be men, they went to their father and said, 'Father, give us each a horse and a sum of money. It is time for us to go out into the world.'

'Oh no, my sons!' said their father. 'I am growing old. Stay with me, that my last years on earth may be free from trouble.'

But no, they would go. They plagued and plagued their father until in the end he had to agree. So they each got from him a fine white horse and a sum of money, and off they went.

When they had gone, Esben said, 'Father, give me also a horse and a sum of money, that I may go out into the world, like my brothers.'

'You are a little fool!' said his father. 'I will give you neither horse nor money. But if I could have kept your brothers at home, and sent *you* away, it would have been better for me in my old age.'

'Well, well,' said Esben, 'I think you will soon be rid of me.'

Since he couldn't get a horse, he went off into the woods and looked among the trees till he found a branch to his liking. And when he had found a branch to his liking, he cut it down, and chopped it and chipped it into the semblance of a horse, leaving four strong twigs for its four legs, a knobby end for its head, and a thin end for its tail. Next, he peeled off the bark and polished the wood till it shone more whitely than his brothers' horses. And having done all that, he got it, and sang out:

'Fly quick, my little stick,
carry me into the world.'

And the stick kicked up the four strong twigs that were its four legs, and galloped away with him after his brothers.

The eleven brothers had been riding gaily along all day; and toward nightfall they came to a great forest. They rode on through the forest, and now it was growing dark. So, seeing a house among the trees, they went to it and knocked at the door.

Out came a frightful old woman, mumbling with her lips, and peering with her eyes. This old woman was a witch, but the brothers didn't know it – and why should eleven lusty young men be afraid of one old woman, however ugly? So they asked if they might lodge there for the night; and she said 'yes', and let them in.

The witch had thirteen daughters, and though

they were not pretty, they were not so very ugly. They waited on the brothers, and the witch cooked them a splendid supper. And after they had supped, they went to bed in a great room, which had twenty-four beds in it: eleven for the brothers and thirteen for the witch's daughters.

Now all this time Esben's little stick had been carrying him along after his brothers. It brought him to the door of the witch's house, and there Esben dismounted, leaned his stick against the door-post, and crept quietly into the house. He went upstairs without anyone seeing him, and hid himself under one of the beds. And there he waited until midnight.

By this time his eleven brothers and the witch's thirteen daughters were all sleeping soundly; and Esben took the nightcaps off his brothers' heads, and the nightcaps off eleven of the witch's daughters; and he put the brothers' nightcaps on the daughters, and the daughters' nightcaps on the brothers. Then he went to hide under the bed again. By and by in came the witch, treading softly as a cat. And she had an axe in her hand. It was so dark that with her bleary old eyes she couldn't see a thing; but she went feeling among the sleepers, and when she felt a man's nightcap she chopped off the head that wore it. And so it came about that she chopped off the heads of eleven of her daughters. And when the eleventh head was off, she crept out again, treading softly as a cat, and well pleased with herself.

And she went to her bed and snored.

As soon as Esben heard the witch snoring he wakened his brothers, and they rose up in terrified haste, escaped from the house, took their horses, and rode off. Did they thank Esben? No, they forgot to do that.

So Esben waited until the sound of their galloping horses dwindled, and then he got astride his little stick, and sang out:

'Fly quick, my little stick,
Carry me after my eleven brothers.'

And the stick kicked up the four twigs that were its four legs, and galloped away with him along the road his brothers had taken.

In the morning the brothers crossed a river and arrived at a king's palace. They asked if they might be taken into service. Yes, they could, if they were content to be stablemen. Otherwise the king had no use for them. So stablemen they became, to look after all the king's horses.

Later in the morning came Esben riding on his

little stick. He, too, asked to be taken into service at the palace. But no-one had any use for *him* – he was but a little fool, they told him. However, the cook took pity on him and gave him some food. He did little jobs for the cook, and the cook was amused by his comical ways and went on giving him food. So he was able to stay on at the palace. And as to his bed – any odd corner would do for that.

Now there was a knight at the palace called Sir Red, who flattered the king and had won his favour. But he was a bad, cruel man, and, except for the king, everyone hated him. Nevertheless, Sir Red, being the king's favourite, gave himself airs. When he strutted about the palace, or out into the grounds, he expected everyone he met to stand at attention for him; and since Esben's eleven brothers saw no reason why they should do this, Sir Red was furious and determined to ruin them. So one day he went to the king and said, 'Those new stablemen of yours are cleverer than you think. I overheard them talking this morning, and they said that if they chose they could get you a wonderful dove, which is all covered with gold and silver feathers: one feather gold, the next silver, the next gold, the next silver, and so on, turn and turn about. But they did not choose to go on such an errand, they said, and would not, unless they were threatened with death.'

The king said, 'I would like to possess such a bird!'

Sir Red said, 'Then send for your stablemen.'

The king sent for the brothers and said, 'I hear you have been boasting that you can get me a dove with feathers of gold and feathers of silver.'

The brothers were astonished. All eleven of them declared that they had never said any such thing. Nor did they believe that such a bird existed.

But the king said, 'Take your choice. I give you three days. Bring me the bird, or lose your heads.'

The brothers went back to their work, lamenting bitterly. Esben found them weeping and wailing, and said, 'What's the matter now?'

'Little fool!' said they. 'What good in telling you? *You* can't help us!'

'Oh, you don't know that,' said Esben. 'I helped you before.'

So in the end they told him how within three days they must get the king a dove with feathers of gold and feathers of silver. Or, if they did not get it, they must lose their heads.

'So lose our heads we shall,' they wailed. 'For there is no such bird in all the world.'

'Oh, you don't know that!' said Esben. 'Give me a bag of peas and perhaps I can help you.'

'Peas, peas, peas!' they cried. 'What good are peas to doomed men? Go away, little fool, and leave us to our misery!'

But Esben wouldn't go away. And at last the brothers gave him a bag of peas to get rid of him.

Esben took the bag of peas, got astride his white stick, and sang out:

'Fly quick, my little stick,
Carry me across the stream.'

Straightaway the stick carried him across the river and into the witch's courtyard; for Esben, whose sharp eyes never missed anything, had noticed that the witch had a dove with alternate gold and silver feathers.

Now he shook the peas out of the bag on to the flagstones of the courtyard, and down fluttered the dove to pick them up. Esben at once caught the dove, put it in the bag, and was astride his stick again before the witch caught sight of him. But just as he was galloping his stick out of the courtyard, the witch saw him, and came running, and shouted after him:

'Is that you, Esben?'

'Ye-e-es!'

'Is it you that has taken my dove?'

'Ye-e-es!'

'Was it you that made me kill my eleven daughters?'

'Ye-e-es!'

'Are you coming again?'

'That may be,' said Esben.

'Then you'll catch it!' shouted the witch.

The stick carried Esben and the dove back to the king's palace. The brothers took the dove to the king. The king was overjoyed to have such a beautiful bird; and in return he gave the brothers both silver and gold. But they never thought of thanking Esben for what he had done for them.

Sir Red was furious. He went to the king and said, 'So, your stablemen have brought you the dove? But that, after all, is not the best they can do. I heard them boasting that they could, if they were so minded, get hold of a boar with tusks of gold and alternate gold and silver bristles.'

The king said, 'I should like to possess such a marvellous boar!' And he sent for the brothers. Said he, 'I hear you have been boasting that you can get hold of a boar with tusks of gold and alternate gold and silver bristles.'

'No, no!' cried the brothers. 'We never boasted of any such thing. Such a boar does not exist on earth!'

‘Take your choice,’ said the king. ‘Bring me that boar within three days, or lose your heads.’

Off went the brothers, lamenting. They sat in the stable among the king’s horses, wailing and beating their breasts. Then came Esben to them.

‘Hullo! What’s the matter here?’

‘Oh! Oh! Oh! What’s the use of telling a little fool like you? *You* can’t help us!’

‘Oh, you don’t know that,’ said Esben. ‘I’ve helped you before.’

So they told him.

And Esben said, ‘Give me a sack of malt, and perhaps I can help you.’

They fetched a sack of malt. Esben took the sack, got astride his white stick, and sang out,

‘Fly quick, my little stick,
Carry me across the stream,’

for he had noticed that the witch possessed such a boar as the king asked for.

Off galloped the stick, over the river and into the witch’s courtyard. There Esben emptied the malt out of the bag. Then came the boar with tusks of gold and alternate gold and silver bristles. The boar was snuffling at the malt, but Esben quickly drew the sack over him, and tied it tight. He was astride his stick again with the sack in his arms before the witch caught sight of him. But, as the stick was galloping out of the courtyard, she came running and shouted:

'Hey, is that you, Esben?'

'Ye-e-es!'

'Is it you that has taken my pretty boar?'

'Ye-e-es!'

'Was it you that took my dove?'

'Ye-e-es!'

'Was it you that made me kill my eleven daughters?'

'Ye-e-es!'

'Are you coming back again?'

'That may be,' said Esben.

'Then you'll catch it!' shouted the witch.

The stick carried Esben and the boar back to the king's palace. The brothers took the boar to the king; but again they forgot to thank Esben for what he had done for them.

The king was delighted with his gold and silver boar; he couldn't make enough of the brothers. He raised them from stablemen to equerries, clothed them in fine garments, and heaped gold and silver on them.

And Sir Red raged in his heart. He went to the king and said, 'What those eleven brothers have done for you is nothing to what they can do. I heard them boasting that, if they were so minded, they could get you a lamp that shines over seven kingdoms.'

The king sent for the brothers and said, 'Get me the lamp that shines over seven kingdoms.'

'But no such lamp exists!' cried the brothers.

The king said, 'As you have boasted, so you must do: or lose your heads.'

The brothers went out lamenting. Then came Esben to them and said, 'Hullo! What's the matter this time?'

'Go away, you little fool,' said the brothers. '*You* can't help us!'

'You might at least tell me,' said Esben. 'I've helped you before.'

So at last they told him, and he said. 'Give me a bushel of salt. It is not impossible that I can help you.'

They fetched him a bushel of salt; and he took the salt, got astride his white stick and sang out:

'Fly quick, my little stick,
Carry me across the stream,'

for he had noticed that the witch had a lamp that shone over seven kingdoms.

The stick carried him over the river and into the witch's courtyard. It was now evening. The witch and her two remaining daughters were in bed.

Esben got on the roof of the house and climbed down the chimney. He searched everywhere for the lamp, but it was one of the witch's greatest treasures. She had hidden it away, and Esben couldn't find it. So he thought, 'I must wait till daylight.' And he crept into the baking oven, which was still warm, intending to sleep there.

He was nearly asleep when he heard the witch calling to one of her daughters, 'I have a powerful hunger on me! Get up, lazy bones, and make me some porridge.'

The daughter got out of bed, lit the fire, and hung a pot filled with water over it.

'Don't put any salt in the porridge!' shouted the witch.

'Neither will I,' said the daughter. She went out into the larder to fetch meal to make the porridge, and Esben slipped out of the oven, and emptied the whole bushel of salt into the pot.

Then he went back to the oven.

The daughter came back, put the meal in the pot, cooked the porridge and carried it up to the witch. The witch tasted it and screamed out, 'You stupid wench! Didn't I say no salt? This muck is as salty as the sea! Go and make me some more!'

'There is no more water in the house,' said the daughter. 'Give me the lamp that shines over seven kingdoms to light me; for I must go to the well.'

'Take it,' said the witch. And she told the daughter where she had hidden the lamp. 'But have a care of it,' she said, 'or you'll catch it!'

So the daughter took the lamp that shone over seven kingdoms, lit it, and went out to the well. And Esben slipped out of the oven and after her. When the daughter got to the well, she set the lamp down on a stone, and stooped over the well to draw up a bucketful of water. Esben gave her a push from behind, she tumbled head first into the well, Esben seized up the lamp, made off with it, and got astride his little white stick.

But the witch heard her daughter screaming and struggling in the well, and she bounded from her bed to pull her out. Then she saw Esben galloping away with the lamp that shone over seven kingdoms, and she shouted after him:

'Hey! Is that you again, Esben?'

'Ye-e-es!'

'Was it you that took my dove?'

'Ye-e-es!'

'And was it you that stole my pretty boar?'

'Ye-e-es!'

'And was it you that made me kill my eleven daughters?'

'Ye-e-es!'

'And have you now taken my lamp and pushed my twelfth daughter into the well?'

'Ye-e-es!'

'Are you coming back again?'

'That may be,' said Esben.

'Then you'll catch it!' shouted the witch.

So Esben took the lamp to his brothers, and his brothers took it to the king. The king was a proud man now: the lamp lit up his whole kingdom, and six other kingdoms as well. He loaded the brothers with gifts and honours; but Esben did not get so much as a word of thanks from them.

It was Sir Red who had to stand at attention

now, when the brothers walked past him with their noses in the air. He was eaten up with jealousy. He couldn't sleep for scheming how to avenge himself.

One day he went to the king and said, 'All that the brothers have done is nothing to what they can do. They are boasting now that they know of a coverlet, hung with golden bells. And this coverlet is so made that if anyone touches it, the bells give out a ring that can be heard over eight kingdoms.'

The king said, 'I would like to possess such a coverlet!' And he sent for the brothers.

Said he, 'You have boasted that you know of a coverlet hung with golden bells whose ring can be heard over eight kingdoms. Get me that coverlet.'

'We cannot get it!' they cried. 'Such a coverlet does not exist on earth!'

'Then you can lose your heads,' said the king.

The brothers went from the king, wailing and lamenting. Then came Esben and said, 'Hullo! What's the matter now?'

'Little fool!' said they. 'You can't even keep yourself in clothes! How can *you* help us?'

'Oh, I don't know that!' said Esben. 'I have helped you before.'

So then they told him about the coverlet. And Esben thought that to get that coverlet would be the very worst errand he had ever set out on, for the coverlet was on the witch's bed. However he could do no worse than fail. So he got astride his white stick, and sang out:

'Fly quick, my little stick,
Carry me across the stream!'

The stick galloped with him across the river and into the witch's courtyard. It was now night. Esben got on to the roof, climbed down the chimney, and crept into the room where the witch was sleeping with the coverlet spread over her. But as soon as he touched the coverlet, the bells gave out a ring that could be heard over eight kingdoms; and the witch bounded up wide awake and caught Esben by the leg.

Esben kicked and struggled. The witch held on to his leg and bawled to her thirteenth daughter, 'Come and help me!' The daughter ran in; they had Esben fast between them; they took him and locked him up in a dark room.

'Now we will fatten him up,' said the witch. 'And when he is fat enough we will eat him.'

It was the thirteenth daughter's task to carry food to Esben, for the twelfth daughter was ill in bed from the fright and the sousing she had got when

Esben pushed her into the well. The thirteenth daughter fed Esben on cream and nut kernels. She was kept busy cracking the nuts for him.

'I am breaking every tooth in my head for you,' she said. 'But I don't mind. You are a brave little fellow, and I have come to like you.'

'Then you don't want me to be cooked and eaten?' said Esben.

'No, I do not,' said she. 'But what can I do?'

One day the witch bade this thirteenth daughter to chop off one of Esben's fingers and bring it to her, that she might see whether he was fattening. The daughter came back to Esben and said, 'I don't want to chop off your finger!'

So Esben told her to take an iron nail and wrap a bit of silk round it, and take that to the witch, who, like all witches, was dimsighted.

The witch bit on the nail and said, 'Ugh! Skinny little beggar! Fatten him up, girl, fatten him up!'

So the daughter took Esben more and more food; and some of it he ate, but most she ate. And Esben got weary of sitting in the dark having nothing to do but eat, and he said, 'Let's make an end of it!'

He bade the daughter bring him some fat and a piece of skin, and he rolled the fat up in the skin in the shape of a finger, and said, 'Take that to your mother.'

The witch bit on the false finger. 'Ah ha!' she cried. 'Now he is fat – so fat that one cannot feel the bone in him! He is ready to be roasted!'

Now it happened that this was the very time when all the witches sailed off on their broomsticks for their yearly gathering on a hill called The Hill of Meeting. If any one of the witches missed this gathering, she was sorely punished by the others, so the witch had to go. Before she went she said to her thirteenth daughter, 'Heat the oven and have Esben ready roasted by the time I come back. See that he is neither overdone nor underdone. If you don't cook him nicely, you'll catch it!'

And she got on her broomstick and off she flew.

The daughter went sniffling and snuffling to Esben, and said, 'Oh what a pity, what a pity! Now I've got to roast you!'

Said Esben, 'If you have to roast me, you have to. Let's get it over!'

So the thirteenth daughter let Esben out of the dark room. And when they were both outside the room, Esben said, 'Oh, I've left my hat in there! I won't be roasted without my hat on my head. You go in and get it for me.'

The thirteenth daughter went back into the dark room; Esben locked the door on her, and left her there. He ran up to the witch's bedroom, seized the coverlet and fled with it into the courtyard, where his little stick was propped against the wall. He got astride the stick and sang out:

'Fly quick, my little stick,
Carry me to the king's palace.'

But the coverlet, as soon as Esben touched it, had given out a ring that could be heard over eight kingdoms. The witch, on her way to The Hill of Meeting, heard the ring, and came flying back home on her broomstick. Her thirteenth daughter was banging on the locked door of the dark room and shouting, 'Let me out!' But the witch paid no attention to *her*! She saw Esben galloping out of the courtyard on his little stick, and she rushed after him, shouting:

'Hey! Is that you again, Esben?'

'Ye-e-es!'

'Is it you that made me kill my eleven daughters?'

'Ye-e-es!'

'And took my dove?'

'Ye-e-es!'

'And my pretty boar?'

'Ye-e-es!'

'And pushed my twelfth daughter into the well, and took my lamp?'

'Ye-e-es!'

'And have now locked my thirteenth daughter in the dark room, and stolen my coverlet?'

'Ye-e-es!'

'Are you coming back again?'

'No, never again,' said Esben.

When she heard that, the witch became so furious that she burst into millions of pieces of flint. The flints strewed the country far and wide, as you can see to this day.

When Esben got back to the king's palace, he found his brothers in a bad way. They had all been thrown into prison, and were going to have their heads cut off on the very next morning, because they had not been able to get the coverlet. But Esben gave the coverlet to the king. The king touched the coverlet, and it gave a ring that could be heard over eight kingdoms. He was happy as could be, thinking how jealous the seven kings of the seven other kingdoms must be feeling. So he let the brothers out of prison. And the brothers at last remembered to thank Esben for all he had done for them.

Then Esben told the king the whole story, and the king ordered Sir Red to be whipped and driven out of the country. And he offered dukedoms to all twelve of the brothers.

But the brothers whispered amongst themselves, and said, 'Truly with such a king it is dukedoms today; but as like as not it will be heads off tomorrow!' And they told the king they would rather go home.

The king, who was chuckling with delight over his dove, and his boar and his lamp and his coverlet, said, 'Let everyone do as he pleases!' And he gave the brothers as much gold and silver as

they could carry to take home with them. So they mounted on their fine white horses, and Esben followed after them on his little white stick, and they all rode back to their parents.

When the father saw his twelve sons coming, he wept for joy. He had never expected to see them again. The brothers now could not make enough of Esben. They told their father how he had five times saved their lives.

The father said, 'So the fool of the family has turned out the best man of you after all!'

And the mother said, 'Didn't I always know it!'

And they rejoiced and held Esben in great esteem ever after.

This story is by Ruth Manning-Sanders.

Hallowe'en

'I'm a Horrifibiter,' said Imran.

'I'm a Fierceychewemup,' said Foxy.

Their eyes glittered dangerously as they stared at each other through the eyeholes in their masks.

'Right, everyone,' called Mr Tucker. 'Clear up every single scrap, please, before you go. I want the paints put away and all this card and polystyrene picked up. If Mrs Beatty comes in here to clean and finds all this rubbish on the floor, she'll turn me into a toad – it is Hallowe'en, after all.'

'You wouldn't be able to teach us, if you were a toad, would you, sir?' said Kevin.

'Ah, but she might turn me into a tiger instead,'

warned Mr Tucker. 'That might make things tricky for you . . . so come on: every scrap cleared up, please.'

Later, Foxy and Imran sauntered along the school road together, wearing their masks. The Horrifibiter was covered in purple warts, and had fearsome horns and a straggly beard. The Fierceychewemup had pointed shark's teeth and an enormous green nose; its woodshaving hair stuck out all round in springy curls. As the two boys walked along, they enjoyed seeing the effect they had on passers-by. A toddler hid its eyes in its mother's skirt; a baby in a pram bounced up and down, dribbling in disbelief; the policeman at the

corner narrowed his eyes and stared back at them; a dog crossed the road to avoid them. But the lollipop lady said:

'Well, hello, Foxy and Imran.'

'How do you know it's us?' asked Foxy in his Fierceychewemup voice.

'I recognize you both by your feet,' she said. 'Imran always wears those stripy socks – and I'd know Foxy's red and black trainers anywhere.'

'But I'm a Fierceychewemup,' roared Foxy.

'And I'm a Horrifibiter,' said Imran

'Very nice, too,' said the lollipop lady. 'And I suppose you'll be out in those masks hallowe'ening tonight?'

'Course,' nodded the two monsters; they liked the idea of padding the streets in disguise.

By six o'clock it was quite dark. A few stars twinkled overhead, and the air smelt of frost. The two boys put on their masks and knocked at Mrs Bell's door. She opened it and stared. The monsters began to chant:

'The sky is blue, the grass is green, have you got a penny for Hallowe'en?'

'Oh, my goodness,' said Mrs Bell. 'What . . . awful creatures. Well, I haven't any pennies for you, but I've just made some gingerbread and it's still warm. Would you like a piece?'

Without waiting for an answer, she went back into the kitchen and brought back two large pieces of gingerbread which she gave to the monsters.

'We used to call Hallowe'en "Mischief Night", when I was young,' she said.

She nodded at them and closed the door. They walked slowly down the path and stood at the gate. They had to push their masks up over their heads so they could eat the gingerbread.

'We forgot to do Trick or Treat,' said Imran with his mouth full.

'We'll do that next,' said Foxy.

They rang the bell at Mr Porrett's door. He opened it and stood there in his shirtsleeves and slippers.

'Trick or treat?' growled the Horrifibiter.

'Trick or treat?' roared the Fierceychewemup.

'Oh, treat, of course,' said Mr Porrett. 'How about treacle toffee?'

He held out a dish he had placed ready by the door, and they each took a large piece.

'Great,' said the Horrifibiter, forgetting to growl.

'Yummy,' said the Fierceychewemup.

They sat on the wall, sucking and chewing, until the toffee was finished. Then they jumped down and crunched their way up Mrs Mundy's drive.

'The sky is blue, the grass is green, have you got a penny for Hallowe'en?'

'Yes,' said Mrs Mundy, 'I thought some Halloweenies might call tonight, so I put some pennies ready. Here you are.'

The two boys held out their hands and she placed a large brown coin on to each of them.

'Now I don't believe in handing out money for you to buy sweets with to rot your teeth,' she said. 'So I'm giving you Victorian bun pennies. You can't spend them, but they're valuable all the same. They're more than a hundred years old. If you look at them carefully, you'll see Queen Victoria on there, wearing her hair in a bun. Goodnight now.'

She shut the door, and the two boys examined the coins under the nearest street lamp. They could just make out the shape of a young woman's head. They slipped the smooth coins into their pockets, and turned into the next drive.

'Colonel Savage lives here,' said Foxy. 'He's got a bulldog.'

'Oh, are you sure we want to call here then?' asked Imran. 'I don't fancy a savage bulldog.'

'No, Wellington's a soft old thing,' said Foxy. 'And he's daft as a brush.'

They walked up to the door and Foxy pulled the cord that hung down by the ship's bell – ding, ding, ding. A face peered out through the round window by the door, then the door opened and Colonel Savage stood there, his red face all smiles.

'I must say I like those masks,' he exclaimed, before they could say anything. 'They remind me of some I saw in South America once. And now I suppose it's Trick or Treat time?'

The monsters nodded.

'Well, I was going to make treacle toffee – that seemed just the thing for Hallowe'en, but Wellington can't manage it without any teeth, you know, so I've made some mulled punch, piping hot, very cheering on a cold night – he likes a saucer of that – I'm quite partial to it myself, of course. Don't worry, there's no alcohol in it, I'm not allowed any – it's mostly fruit juice and cinnamon, but none the worse for that.'

He disappeared into the kitchen and the boys stared at Wellington's scowling face. Then Colonel Savage reappeared with two steaming mugs. The monsters pushed their masks up again and sipped the drink; it was hot and spicy.

'Mmm, delish,' said the Horrifibiter.

They finished their drinks, gave Wellington a nervous pat and said goodbye.

'I'm feeling quite full up,' said Fierceychewemup.

'Let's do just one more,' said the Horrifibiter.

'Oh, all right – this is Mrs Reed's house,' said Foxy. 'She's really nice.'

They pulled their masks down over their faces and rang the doorbell. Mrs Reed stood there, wiping her hands on her apron. The light from the hall shone down on them.

'The sky is blue, the grass is green, have you got a penny for Hallowe'en?'

'Certainly not!' exclaimed Mrs Reed. 'I'm not having cheeky youngsters begging for money on my doorstep – be off with you.'

'Er . . . Trick or Treat then?' asked Imran, backing away.

'You'll get no treats from me, young man, coming here in nasty masks, frightening a poor old woman in the dark!'

The door slammed shut.

'I thought you said she was nice,' said Imran.

'She is usually,' said Foxy.

'I'm going to play a trick on her,' said Imran.

'Oh, no, Immy,' said Foxy. 'She *is* nice, honest, and she's a friend of ours.'

'Just a *little* trick,' insisted Imran.

He took a piece of chalk from his pocket and tiptoed to the wall near the front door. Along the bricks he scrawled:

'Mrs Reed is a real old meanie,
She wouldn't give a treat to a Halloweenie.'

'Hang on, Immy,' said Foxy. 'You can't leave that there.'

'Keep your hair on,' said Imran. 'The rain'll wash it off in no time. Now, shall we do some more houses?'

Foxy shook his head. He'd had enough for one night.

'See you Monday then,' called Imran. 'Bye,' and he ran off to his end of the street.

The following morning, just as Foxy was finishing his breakfast, there was a knock at the door. His mother went to answer it. He could hear the murmur of voices and his mother saying, 'Of course, of course.'

'That was Mrs Reed,' she said, coming back into the room.

Foxy swallowed his cereal the wrong way and choked. His mother thumped him on the back and went on:

'She says there's a little job she'd particularly like you to do for her, Foxy – so I said you'd pop round before doing my shopping, to see what she wants.'

Foxy forced himself to ring at Mrs Reed's front door. He kept his face turned away from the chalked scrawl on the bricks. He felt quite sick.

'Ah, Foxy,' smiled Mrs Reed. 'Just the sort of sensible lad I need. Do you see this?'

She waved her hand towards the chalked words.

'A couple of young vandals visited me last night; they had masks on, so I couldn't see their faces, unfortunately. It was Mischief Night, you see, and when I refused to give them a treat, this is what they left me.'

Foxy scuffed the toe of his trainer on the step. Mrs Reed went on:

'Now you know I often get twinges of rheumatism, so I thought it would be easier for someone with young muscles to clean it off. Here's a bucket of hot water, and here's some cleaning powder and a scrubbing brush – ring the bell when you've finished, and I'll come out and see what sort of a job you've made of it.'

Foxy was left with no choice in the matter. He scrubbed and scrubbed at the writing, poured scouring powder on to the brush and scrubbed away again until he was sweating all over with the effort. Eventually all the writing was rubbed off. Then he had to rinse the streaks of white powder off the bricks. His wet hands were red and sore in the biting wind. He rang Mrs Reed's doorbell and could hear her limping to open it.

'Ah, Foxy,' she said, looking at the wall, which was now dripping wet, but clean. 'You are a good boy; thank you very much. Now here's a bag of apples off my tree, I'm sure your family can make good use of them. Watch how you go now. Don't trip; your laces are undone.'

She smiled to herself as Foxy put down the bag of apples and bent to do up his laces.

'Do you know, Foxy,' she said, 'I'd recognize those red and black trainers anywhere.'

This story is by Margaret Joy.

What the Neighbours Did

Mum didn't like the neighbours, although – as we were the end cottage of the row – we only had one, really: Dirty Dick. Beyond him, the Macys.

Dick lived by himself – they said there used to be a wife, but she'd run away years ago; so now he lived as he wanted, which Mum said was like a pig in a pig-sty. Once I told Mum that I envied him, and she blew me up for it. Anyway, I'd have liked some of the things he had. He had two cars, although not for driving. He kept rabbits in one, and hens roosted in the other. He sold the eggs, which made part of his living. He made the rest from dealing in old junk (and in the village they

said that he'd a stocking full of gold sovereigns which he kept under the mattress of his bed). Mostly he went about on foot, with his handcart for the junk; but he also rode a tricycle. The boys used to jeer at him sometimes, and once I asked him why he didn't ride a bicycle like everyone else. He said he liked a tricycle because you could go as slowly as you wanted, looking at things properly, without ever falling off.

Mrs Macy didn't like Dirty Dick any more than my mum did, but then she disliked everybody anyway. She didn't like Mr Macy. He was retired, and every morning in all weathers Mrs Macy'd turn him out into the garden and lock the door against him and make him stay there until he'd done as much work as she thought right. She'd put his dinner out to him through the scullery window. She couldn't bear anything alive about the place (you couldn't count old Macy himself, Dad used to say). That was one of the reasons why she didn't think much of us, with our dog and cat and Nora's two love-birds in a cage. Dirty Dick's hens and rabbits were even worse, of course.

Then the affair of the yellow dog made the Macys really hate Dirty Dick. It seems that old Mr Macy secretly got himself a dog. He never had any money of his own, because his wife made him hand it over, every week; so Dad reckoned that he must have begged the dog off someone who'd otherwise have had it destroyed.

The dog began as a secret, which sounds just about impossible, with Mrs Macy around. But every day Mr Macy used to take his dinner and eat it in his tool-shed, which opened on the side furthest from the house. That must have been his temptation; but none of us knew he'd fallen into it, until one summer evening we heard a most awful screeching from the Macys' house.

'That's old Ma Macy screaming,' said Dad,

spreading his bread and butter.

'Oh, dear!' said Mum, jumping up and then sitting down again. 'Poor old Mr Macy!' But Mum was afraid of Mrs Macy. 'Run upstairs, boy, and see if you can see what's going on.'

So I did. I was just in time for the excitement, for, as I leaned out of the window, the Macys' back door flew open. Mr Macy came out first with his head down and his arms sort of curved above it; and Mrs Macy came out close behind him, aiming at his head with a light broom – but aiming quite hard. She was screeching words, although it was difficult to pick out any of them. But some words came again and again, and I began to follow: Mr Macy had brought hairs with him into the house – short, curly, yellowish hairs, and he'd left those hairs all over the upholstery, and they must have come from a cat or a dog or a hamster or I don't know what, and so on and so on. Whatever the creature was, he'd been keeping it in the tool-shed, and turn it out he was going to, this very minute.

As usual, Mrs Macy was right about what Mr Macy was going to do.

He opened the shed-door and out ambled a dog – a big, yellowy-white old dog, looking a bit like a sheep, somehow, and about as quick-witted. As though it didn't notice what a tantrum Mrs Macy was in, it blundered gently towards her, and she lifted her broom high, and Mr Macy covered his eyes; and then Mrs Macy let out a real scream – a plain shriek – and dropped the broom and shot indoors and slammed the door after her.

The dog seemed puzzled, naturally; and so was I. It lumbered around towards Mr Macy, and then I saw its head properly, and that it had the most extraordinary eyes – like headlamps, somehow. I don't mean as big as headlamps, of course, but with a kind of whitish glare to them. Then I realized that the poor old thing must be blind.

The dog had raised its nose inquiringly towards Mr Macy, and Mr Macy had taken one timid, hopeful step towards the dog, when one of the sash-windows of the house went up and Mrs Macy leaned out. She'd recovered from her panic, and she gave Mr Macy his orders. He was to take that disgusting animal and turn it out into the road, where he must have found it in the first place.

I knew that old Macy would be too dead scared to do anything else but what his wife told him.

I went down again to where the others were having tea.

'Well?' said Mum.

I told them, and I told them what Mrs Macy was

making Mr Macy do to the blind dog. 'And if it's turned out like that on the road, it'll be killed by the first car that comes along.'

There was a pause, when even Nora seemed to be thinking; but I could see from their faces what they were thinking.

Dad said at last: 'That's bad. But we've four people in this little house, and a dog already, and a cat and two birds. There's no room for anything else.'

'But it'll be killed.'

'No,' said Dad. 'Not if you go at once, before any car comes, and take that dog down to the village, to the police-station. Tell them it's a stray.'

'But what'll they do with it?'

Dad looked as though he wished I hadn't asked that, but he said: 'Nothing, I expect. Well, they might hand it over to the Cruelty to Animals people.'

'And what'll *they* do with it?'

Dad was rattled. 'They do what they think best for animals – I should have thought they'd have taught you that at school. For goodness sake, boy!'

Dad wasn't going to say any more, nor Mum, who'd been listening with her lips pursed up. But everyone knew that the most likely thing was that an old, blind, ownerless dog would be destroyed.

But anything would be better than being run over and killed by a car just as you were sauntering along in the evening sunlight; so I started out of the house after the dog.

There he was, sauntering along, just as I'd imagined him. No sign of Mr Macy, of course: he'd have been called back indoors by his wife.

As I ran to catch up with the dog, I saw Dirty

Dick coming home, and nearer the dog than I was. He was pushing his handcart, loaded with the usual bits of wood and other junk. He saw the dog coming and stopped, and waited; the dog came on hesitantly towards him.

'I'm coming for him,' I called.

'Ah,' said Dirty Dick. 'Yours?' He held out his hand towards the dog – the hand that my mother always said she could only bear to take hold of if the owner had to be pulled from certain death in a quicksand. Anyway, the dog couldn't see the colour of it, and it positively seemed to like the smell; it came on.

'No,' I said. 'Macys were keeping it, but Mrs Macy turned it out. I'm going to take it down to the police as a stray. What do you think they'll do with it?'

Dirty Dick never said much; this time he didn't answer. He just bent down to get his arm round the dog and in a second he'd hoisted him up on top of all the stuff in the cart. Then he picked up the handles and started off again.

So the Macys saw the blind dog come back to the row of cottages in state, as you might say, sitting on top of half a broken lavatory-seat on the very pinnacle of Dirty Dick's latest load of junk.

Dirty Dick took good care of his animals, and

he took good care of this dog he adopted. It always looked well-fed and well-brushed. Sometimes he'd take it out with him, on the end of a long string; mostly he'd leave it comfortably at home. When it lay out in the back-garden, old Mr Macy used to look longingly over the fence. Once or twice I saw him poke his fingers through, towards what had once been *his* dog. But that had been for only a very short, dark time in the shed; and the old dog never moved towards the fingers. Then, 'Macy!' his terrible old wife would call from the house, and he'd have to go.

Then suddenly we heard that Dirty Dick had

been robbed – old Macy came round specially to tell us. 'An old sock stuffed with pound notes, that he kept up the bedroom chimney. Gone. Hasn't he *told* you?'

'No,' said Mum, 'but we don't have a lot to do with him.' She might have added that we didn't have a lot to do with the Macys either – I think this was the first time I'd ever seen one step over our threshold in a neighbourly way.

'You're thick with him sometimes,' said old Macy, turning on me. 'Hasn't he told *you* all about it?'

'Me?' I said. 'No.'

'Mind you, the whole thing's not to be wondered at,' said the old man. 'Front and back doors never locked, and money kept in the house. That's a terrible temptation to anyone with a weakness that way. A temptation that shouldn't have been put.'

'I daresay,' said Mum. 'It's a shame, all the same. His savings.'

'Perhaps the police'll be able to get it back for him,' I said. 'There'll be clues.'

The old man jumped – a nervous sort of jump. 'Clues? You think the police will find clues? I never thought of that. No, I did not. But has he gone to the police, anyway, I wonder. That's what I wonder. That's what I'm asking you.' He paused, and I realized that he meant me again. 'You're thick with him, boy. Has he gone to the police? That's what I want to know. . .'

His mouth seemed to have filled with saliva, so that he had to stop to swallow, and couldn't say more. He was in a state, all right.

At that moment Dad walked in from work and wasn't best pleased to find that visitor instead of his tea waiting; and Mr Macy went.

Dad listened to the story over tea, and across the fence that evening he spoke to Dirty Dick and said he was sorry to hear about the money.

'Who told you?' asked Dirty Dick.

Dad said that old Macy had told us. Dirty Dick just nodded; he didn't seem interested in talking about it any more. Over that weekend no police came to the row, and you might have thought that old Macy had invented the whole thing, except that Dirty Dick had not contradicted him.

On Monday I was rushing off to school when I saw Mr Macy in their front garden, standing just between a big laurel bush and the fence. He looked straight at me and said 'Good morning' in a kind of whisper. I don't know which was odder – the whisper, or his wishing me a good morning. I answered in rather a shout, because I was late and hurrying past. His mouth had opened as though he meant to say more, but then it shut, as though he'd changed his mind. That was all, that morning.

The next morning he was in just the same spot again, and hailed me in the same way; and this time I was early, so I stopped.

He was looking shiftily about him, as though someone might be spying on us: but at least his wife couldn't be doing that, because the laurel bush was between him and their front windows. There was a tiny pile of yellow froth at one corner of his mouth, as though he'd been chewing his words over in advance. The sight of the froth made me want not to stay; but then the way he looked at me made me feel that I had to. No, it just made me; I had to.

'Look what's turned up in our back-garden,' he said, in the same whispering voice. And he held up a sock so dirty – partly with soot – and so smelly that it could only have been Dirty Dick's. It was stuffed full of something – pound notes, in fact. Old Macy's story of the robbery had been true in every detail.

I gaped at him.

'It's all to go back,' said Mr Macy. 'Back exactly to where it came from.' And then, as though I'd suggested the obvious – that he should hand the sock back to Dirty Dick himself with the same explanation just given to me: 'No, no. It must go back as though it had never been – never been taken away.' He couldn't use the word 'stolen'. 'Mustn't have the police poking round us. Mrs Macy wouldn't like it.' His face twitched at his own mention of her; he leaned forward. 'You must put it back, boy. Put it back for me and keep your mouth shut. Go on. Yes.'

He must have been half out of his mind to think that I should do it, especially as I still didn't twig why. But as I stared at his twitching face I suddenly did understand. I mean, that old Macy had taken the sock, out of spite, and then lost his nerve.

He must have been half out of his mind to think that I would do that for him; and yet I did it. I took the sock and put it inside my jacket and turned back to Dirty Dick's cottage. I walked boldly up to the front door and knocked, and of course there was no answer. I knew he was already out with the cart.

There wasn't a sign of anyone looking, either from our house or the Macys'. (Mr Macy had already disappeared.) I tried the door and it opened, as I knew it would. I stepped inside and closed it behind me.

I'd never been inside before. The house was dirty, I suppose, and smelt a bit, but not really badly. It smelt of Dirty Dick and hens and rabbits –

although it was untrue that he kept either hens or rabbits indoors, as Mrs Macy said. It smelt of dog, too, of course.

Opening straight off the living-room, where I stood, was a twisty, dark little stairway – exactly as in our cottage next door.

I went up.

The first room upstairs was full of junk. A narrow passageway had been kept clear to the second room, which opened off the first one. This was Dirty Dick's bedroom, with the bed unmade, as it probably was for weeks on end.

There was the fire-place, too, with a good deal of soot which had recently been brought down from the chimney. You couldn't miss seeing that – Dirty Dick couldn't have missed it, at the time. Yet he'd done nothing about his theft. In fact, I realized now that he'd probably said nothing either. The only person who'd let the cat out of the bag was poor old Macy himself.

I'd been working this out as I looked at the fire-place, standing quite still. Round me the house was silent. The only sound came from outside, where I could see a hen perched on the bumper of the old car in the back garden, clucking for an egg newly laid. But when she stopped, there came another, tiny sound that terrified me: the click of a front-gate opening. Feet were clumping up to the front door . . .

I stuffed the sock up the chimney again, any old how, and was out of that bedroom in seconds; but on the threshold of the junk-room I stopped, fixed by the headlamp glare of the blind dog. He must have been there all the time, lying under a three-legged washstand, on a heap of rags. All the time he would have been watching me, if he'd had his eyesight. He didn't move.

Meanwhile the front door had opened and the footsteps had clumped inside, and stopped. There was a long pause, while I stared at the dog, who stared at me; and down below Dirty Dick listened and waited – he must have heard my movement just before.

At last: 'Well,' he called, 'why don't you come down?'

There was nothing else to do but go. Down that dark, twisty stair, knowing that Dirty Dick was waiting for me at the bottom. He was a big man, and strong. He heaved his junk about like nobody's business.

But when I got down, he wasn't by the foot of the stairs; he was standing by the open door, looking out, with his back to me. He hadn't been surprised to hear someone upstairs in his house, uninvited; but when he turned round from the doorway, I could see that he hadn't expected to see *me*. He'd expected someone else – old Macy, I suppose.

I wanted to explain that I'd only put the sock back – there was soot all over my hands, plain to be seen, of course – and that I'd had nothing to do with taking it in the first place. But he'd drawn his thick brows together as he looked at me, and he jerked his head towards the open door. I was frightened, and I went past him without saying anything. I was late for school now, anyway, and I ran.

I didn't see Dirty Dick again.

Later that morning Mum chose to give him a talking to, over the back fence, about locking his doors against pilferers in future. She says he didn't say he would, he didn't say he wouldn't; and he didn't say anything about anything having been stolen, or returned.

Soon after that, Mum saw him go out with the hand-cart with all his rabbits in a hutch, and he came back later without them. He did the same with his hens. We heard later that he'd given them away in the village; he hadn't even bothered to try to sell them.

Then he went round to Mum, wheeling the

tricycle. He said he'd decided not to use it any-more, and I could have it. He didn't leave any message for me.

Later still, Mum saw him set off for the third time that day with his hand-cart: not piled very high even, but the old dog was sitting on top. And that was the last anyone saw of him.

He must have taken very little money with him: they found the sooty sock, still nearly full, by the rent-book on the mantelpiece. There was plenty to pay the rent due and to pay for cleaning up the house and the garden for the next tenant. He must have been fed up with being a householder, Dad said – and with having neighbours. He just wanted to turn tramp, and he did.

It was soon after he'd gone that I said to Mum that I envied him, and she blew me up, and went on and on about soap and water and fecklessness. All the same, I did envy him. I didn't even have the fun with his tricycle that he'd had. I never rode it, although I wanted to, because I was afraid that people I knew would laugh at me.

This story is by Philippa Pearce.